MY VAMPIRE, MY KING

MARGY MILLET

TRUE DIRECTIONS
AN AFFILIATE OF TARCHER BOOKS

iUniverse®

MY VAMPIRE, MY KING

iUniverse books may be ordered through booksellers or by contacting:

iUniverse
1663 Liberty Drive
Bloomington, IN 47403
www.iuniverse.com
1-800-Authors (1-800-288-4677)

ISBN: 978-1-4917-6365-0 (sc)
ISBN: 978-1-4917-6366-7 (e)

Print information available on the last page.

iUniverse rev. date: 3/27/2015

CONTENTS

PROLOGUE

ELENA MADE IT TO her house in just ten minutes. Her father had sounded so desperate on the phone. As she rushed into the house, she detected the thick, metallic smell of blood. "Dad," she called. She didn't get an answer. "Dad," she called out louder.

"Up here," she heard him gasp weakly.

She ran upstairs to her parents' room. The door was wide open. She turned to where the scent was coming from and saw her father sitting up in bed. She ran to him, kneeling in front of him. "Oh my God, Dad what happened?" she wailed.

"Arnav's men found me," he said as blood splattered from his mouth.

"Don't speak," she murmured with tears rolling down her face. "I'll get a cloth," she said moving toward the bathroom.

"No, we don't have time."

"What do you mean? What's going on?"

He started to say something, but instead he coughed up a bit more blood. Elena moved with vampire speed to the bathroom and got a wet washcloth. As she gently cleaned his mouth with the cloth, her father grabbed her hand and took the cloth from her. "Honey, sit," he ordered.

She looked at him for a few seconds then sat down next to him. He dropped the cloth on the bed and took one of her hands between his.

"Listen carefully," he said in a low voice.

"Dad, we can talk later. Let me take care of you," she whispered.

He took a strand of her hair in his hand and softly caressed it.

"I've always loved your hair. I remember many times trying to comb the tangles out of it, then putting it in a braid."

"Dad, please."

"Elena stop. Listen to me."

She wanted to say more but remained silent as he asked. He coaxed her head with his hand and settled it on his shoulder. Elena held his hand tightly.

"I have to go. If the Arnav finds out I have a family, he will stop at nothing to hurt you all. No one can know you and your sister are half Fae—ever." he whispered.

He let go of her, yanked the pendant necklace from his neck, then took one of her hands and dropped it onto her palm.

"Hold on to this. If you are ever confronted with one of my people, show them this. They will know you're my blood."

"Dad, no," she said pushing the pendant towards him.

"Elena, this has been in my family for generations. It's yours now." He was barely able to utter these words when another bout of coughing stopped him. She held on to him tightly; his whole body was trembling now.

"In the strongbox you'll find money and documents for another house. Move the family away from the Arkady vicinity. You're older now, if he finds out about you he'll take you from your mother and sister. Do everything possible to prevent that from happening."

She just stared at him. He tugged at her chin with his fingers, forcing her to look at him, "Do you understand?"

"Elena," he yelled, "Do you understand?"

"Yes."

"I have to go. Everything you need is in the strongbox."

She slid off the bed and helped him stand up. He wrapped her in his arms, holding on to her for a few minutes. Then he stepped back and together they slowly walked out of the bedroom and down the stairs into the kitchen. He stopped and moved away from her, giving her a big smile. "Go get your mom and sister, then don't waste any time moving the family to the new house."

"Dad..." she interrupted him.

He stopped her from talking by raising his hand. "Elena, do as I say, please. Everything is explained in the documents."

"Okay," she said with more tears rolling down her cheeks. "Let me get you to where you're going."

"No, it's safer if I go alone. I'm going to be fine."

"Dad," she murmured.

"Go to your mom and sister. Take care of them."

"I will."

"I love you honey," he said hugging her one last time.

"I love you too."

He opened the back door and walked out. She started to follow him, "No, don't follow me. Get Iskra and Ayla, find the strongbox, and follow the instructions in the documents. Goodbye sweetie," he said stepping out into the darkness and breaking into a fast run toward the woods.

Elena stood at the open door for a few minutes, then closed the door and locked it. She walked out of the kitchen, down the hall, and out of the house. Slowly and calmly, not wanting to attract any attention, she got into her car and drove away.

She got the strongbox and followed her father instructions to the letter. The box contained all the documents she needed to uproot her family and spirit them away to a new life. She never considered doing anything else.

Chapter One

Ten Years Later

Elena discreetly looked around the airport for any signs that she had been followed. Slowly, she walked towards the baggage-claim area. She stood there in the middle of the crowd, trying to fit in as she waited for her baggage to come out. After waiting for some time, she spotted her two bags and quickly pulled both of them off the conveyor belt.

She moved very cautiously, trying not to bring any attention to herself. She pulled the handles out and tipped the luggage on the rollers as she walked out of the airport building. It was still dark outside but she knew dawn would be approaching soon. She quickly found the pickup stop where she could catch the van that would take her to the car rental location. She got in the van and sat down, observing everyone around her. She got her car and drove off towards what could possibly be her last event planner assignment——an assignment forced on her by her pack leader who was cruel, vindictive and heartless. She knew she had to do the job because her family's lives depended on it.

She closed her eyes and took a deep breath, letting it out slowly. She remembered her life back in Russia, full of bumps and obstacles and so many secrets, but no matter what life had thrown at her, she was able to succeed. Now with this assignment she could lose her life, or worse, the lives of her family. She hated that Arnav literally twisted her arm to take this job. Elena didn't put much value on her own life, but she was going to make sure her family survived.

She put some music on and focused on her driving. The drive would be long but it would give her the time she needed to go over her plan again. Right now, she needed to find a place to rest before daylight came. She knew she had maybe two hours before dawn. She used the car's GPS to locate a nearby motel. She drove to the motel and got a room, making sure to pay for everything in cash. When she got to her room, she took a quick shower and got settled in for the day.

Elena knew she only had two months to carry out her orders or her mother and sister would be killed. She went over the plan in her head again and again. She kept thinking about the exact moment she had come face to face with him. For every event that she planned, she always tried very hard to keep away from him. But when her agency won the bid on the king's mating ceremony, they offered her this great opportunity. She hadn't expected the leader of her vampire pack to find out about her hidden family after ten years.

Elena yawned; the daylight drowsiness took over her and in minutes she was asleep.

She woke up startled. She looked around for a moment forgetting where she was. The sun was just going down, and small strips of yellow and orange were still visible on the horizon. She threw the sheet off her body and sat at the edge of bed. She couldn't believe she was here when, just a month before she was sitting behind her desk in her office happily working on a plan for an event when the leader of her pack walked in. He ordered her to take the vampire king's event. He hinted, in a not-so-subtle way, that certain people that she knew and loved would get hurt. He even casually mentioned an address in Russia, proving that he knew where they were. But how did he find out? She shook her head, slid out of bed, and walked in to the bathroom. She took a quick shower and got dressed, thinking about the two hours she still had to drive.

She returned the keys to the manager and left the motel. After almost two hours of driving, she saw the exit to Leesville, Louisiana, the home of the vampire king and her home for the next two months— quite likely her last home. She took the exit and drove for another twenty minutes. It was just dusk now. At her next turn, she reached her destination and found herself in front of a thirty-foot-high metal gate.

"Holy shit," she murmured to herself.

She took a deep breath, lowered the window and spoke to the guard at the gate. She gave him her credentials and showed her ID. He instructed another guard to open the gate and let her in. Elena took the driveway to the front of a huge mansion. As she parked the car in front of the house, a servant came out. She got out of the car, grabbed her carry case and went to the back of the car to open the trunk. The servant pulled out the two suitcases and rolled them towards the house. "This way, my lady," he said walking in front of her.

She could see that the servant was human, which didn't surprise her because most vampires have humans helping them, especially during the day while they slept. She followed the man into the house. "This way to your room," he said turning to her.

She thanked him and smiled before following him up a set of stairs, then down a long hall. He opened a bedroom door for her and followed her into the room with her baggage.

She looked around the room in confusion, "I think this may be an error. I'm here to work; I'm not a guest."

"I was instructed to give you this room, my lady," he said bowing to her.

"Oh, okay. Please call me Elena," she said as she took in her surroundings.

"If you need anything, you just need to pick up the phone on the nightstand and call," he said before closing the door.

Elena was left standing alone in the middle of this huge room. It was bigger than her entire apartment back in Russia. She walked around checking out everything. She pulled her phone out and sent a quick text message to her sister. She knew it was early in Russia, but her sister would get it when she woke up.

She grabbed her bag from the corner and pulled a folder out. She opened it and looked at the documents the agency had given her with the information for this event. She read through the papers, noticing that there was no picture of the king and his bride to be inside. She took a deep breath and snapped the folder close.

She was on edge right now and felt that she needed to expend some energy. She had plenty of time before meeting with the king and his mate, so she decided to exercise—that always worked for her. Maybe there was a training room or some kind of gym. She pulled her exercising clothes out and put them on, then walked down the long hall and back down the stairs. There was no one around to ask for information, so she decided to investigate herself and turned down a long hall.

She walked for a few minutes and then heard the sound of banging, almost like punching behind a closed door. She followed the sound until she was facing the door. She opened the door and saw the biggest training room ever. There was equipment everywhere: one wall was full of weapons; the opposite side of the room was full of all kinds of exercise equipment.

In the far corner of the room, a man was working out with the punching bag. She looked him over and noticed that he was wearing just sweatpants and no shirt. He was probably a foot or so taller than her and she considered herself tall at five foot seven. His upper body was formed in a fabulous V-shape; his shoulders were broad and wide, his stomach was lean and his arms were like two huge logs. He was moving around the bag, deftly punching and weaving.

Elena could feel his eyes on her as he lost his focus and missed a punch, but immediately caught himself and got back his rhythm. He continued with the workout as she pretended to ignore him completely. She walked over to the wall and leisurely checked out all the weapons— it was an extensive collection. She didn't even hear him move until he was right by her side. "Hi," he said with a big smile.

Now that he was right in front of her he seemed even taller. She had to look up at him to see his face. Her head just made it up to his muscle-bound chest. She shook her head and took a step back from him. He seemed to be waiting for something as he just stood there in front of her, she didn't know what. "Hi," he said again.

"Sorry, hi."

"You're new here," he observed.

"Yes," she simply answered.

"A woman of few words."

"I guess."

She looked at him as he looked over her whole body. Her body reacted strangely to his stare, and even stranger, her heart beat faster. This had never happened to her before. She didn't consider herself attractive in the least and she was always so serious that men never approached her or showed any interest in her. "I didn't know there would be anyone here so early; usually everyone is feeding," he said moving closer.

"Well, I'm not like everyone," she said.

"I can see that."

Sebastian looked her up and down brazenly, taking in what she looked like and what she was wearing: a skimpy sports bra accentuated the curves of her full breasts, and a small pair of boy cut shorts just barely covered her beautifully round butt, which was attached to very nicely defined legs. She could tell that he appreciated what he saw as his gaze lingered on her body.

He hesitated for a moment then introduced himself by his nickname. "I'm Bash."

"Elena."

"You want to spar with me, hand to hand?" he asked.

"Sure."

She followed him to the large mats and stretched her muscles a bit before turning to face him. She got in a fighting stance with her hands in front of her. With swift, controlled moves they tentatively took the measure of each other, circling around before attacking. Elena threw several combination punches. Her moves were precise and solid. She forced him to defend himself. They were sparring with each other for more than an hour when she swiftly kicked him off his feet and flipped him over landing right in top of him. He couldn't move; their breath was coming fast and short. Instantly there was a charge of energy running through their bodies. Her breasts were just above his face and she watched as his gaze came up further to see that she was watching him too. She was half kneeling on his chest. His eyes moved back to her breasts as a drop of sweat ran down from her collarbone to her cleavage. He kicked his legs up and flipped her over—now he was on top, holding her arms over her head with his lower body tightly holding her legs down on the mat. "Get off me," she said firmly, looking him right in the eyes.

He smiled at her but didn't move. "Get off," she yelled, struggling to loosen her arms.

Her eyes sparked with authentic anger so he quickly let her go. He stood up straight and moved a few steps away from her. She stood up and took a step back too. She stared at him and he didn't take his eyes away from her. "Thank you," he said moving forward and stretching his hand out to her.

Elena hesitated for a moment but then stretched her hand out too. As their hands touched, an amazing charge of energy ran through her body settling between her thighs. She had never felt that before. Quickly, she pulled her hand away from his and rubbed it on her thigh while taking a few more steps away from him.

"How about tomorrow, same time?" he said smiling to her.

She hesitated for a moment then said, "Sure," as she turned around and walked towards the gym door. She could feel his gaze on her as she exited.

Elena rushed out of the gym. Her heart was beating fast and her body was feeling strange, almost electrified. The energy she felt going through her body when they touched was amazing. As she turned a corner, she nearly walked into the same servant who had welcomed her into the mansion just hours ago.

"My lady."

"Elena, please."

"Elena. There's a meeting in the living room. They're waiting for you."

"Oh, I'll be there in ten," she said quickly rushing up the stairs and down the hall into her room.

Elena got showered and dressed in record time. She walked downstairs where she found the servant waiting for her in the foyer. "This way," the servant said.

He walked her into a living room where there were several people talking. She stood behind the servant not moving or looking at anyone in particular. "Master, this is Miss Baich."

"Thank you, Matthew."

The man who the servant addressed as "Master" turned around. He didn't say anything but just stared at her, as did the rest of the group. Elena took a small breath and stood still as this man checked her out. *So this is the Vampire King*, she thought. *This is the man Arnav wants me to assassinate.*

"Miss Baich," he said offering his hand.

"Mr. Hunter," she said, firmly shaking his hand.

"Please excuse us," he said to the group as he walked out of the room. Elena followed a couple of feet behind him. He walked into what looked like an office and she walked in after him. He moved behind a huge mahogany desk then motioned her to sit down in a chair in front of it. "Please sit."

He sat down and opened a folder on the desk. He read for a few seconds then put the folder down. He looked at her and said, "You weren't expected until two weeks from now."

"Yes I know, but I was able to complete my previous project sooner than expected so I decided to come early. I hope that's not a problem."

"No, not at all. We appreciate your agency's quick response to our request for your services. You come with very high credentials."

"Thank you."

"Your proposal is extraordinary. I believe you have the unique qualities we require for this ceremony."

"Thanks. I'm glad that I have more than a month to prepare for the ceremony, so I can make this event a memorable one for everyone."

"Yes, it's great timing on your part. You will be working directly with me. You will only discuss any matter concerning this event with me."

"Of course," she agreed.

"How about if we start tomorrow night? Tonight, why don't you enjoy some time off."

"Thank you," she said.

He got up out of the chair and walked to the front of the desk as she stood up. He walked her out of the room then back to the main foyer. "By the way, you won't be needing the rental car. I'll have one of my men return it tomorrow. We have many cars in the garage for your use." he said.

"Sure, the paperwork is in the glove compartment."

"See you tomorrow," he said then turned around and walked back down the hall to his office.

"Tomorrow," she said as she stood in the foyer by herself.

CHAPTER TWO

ELENA STOOD ALONE IN the foyer for a few seconds longer. She felt closed in and needed some fresh air. She walked to the front door and then went outside where she saw a stone walkway leading into a garden. The weather was fantastic; it was warm but not muggy. There was a small breeze coming through the trees. She continued walking until she found a small bench where she sat down and pulled her phone from her blazer pocket. There was a text message from her sister. She responded to the message and put the phone back in her pocket. She closed her eyes and a tear rolled down her cheek, which she wiped away with the back of her hand. Could she obey her leader and go on with this horrendous plan? Could she kill the vampire king and save her family too?

She held her head in her hands and took several deep breaths, then got up and walked back toward the mansion where she found an open door. She walked inside and discovered she was in the living room where she had met the king earlier. She walked through the room and went to look for food. She found Matthew walking down the hall. "Matthew, right?"

"Yes."

"Can you please show me to the supply of blood? I'm due for my feeding."

"Sure," he said turning around and walking ahead of her.

Elena caught up to him and walked by his side. They entered a huge kitchen and he led her to a pantry and showed her the refrigerator that held the blood supply.

"Thanks."

She took one of the bags out and found a cup inside the cabinet. Sitting down at the kitchen table in the corner, she slowly savored the blood. Back home, she had to get blood from the butcher. She and the butcher's son were best friends in school. He was one of the few vampires she cared for a lot. It was quiet in the kitchen and she was glad to be alone. There was so much on her mind, including her unusual reaction to the vampire in the gym.

Back in the study, Sebastian was pacing back and forth in front of Julian. The report stating that there may be an attempt on his life at the mating ceremony had just reached his ears and he was going over the report that had recently arrived from his source. The source was trustworthy so they knew to take it seriously. He couldn't believe that any of his leaders would want to have him killed. He considered himself a fair and just king. The report specified that it would be a professional assassin, but there were no suspects as yet. They spent another several minutes going over the report and then Julian changed the subject, "I met with the mating ceremony planner."

"You did? She's early."

"Yes, a very pretty lady."

"Really," he said hardly paying attention to his brother.

"Hey, where is your head tonight?" asked Julian.

"Oh, sorry. Do you know if we hired a new guard or something?"

"No, all new hires go through me. Why?"

Sebastian remembered Elena's gorgeous breasts in his face, her luscious hips and thighs tight against his stomach. How could it be possible that, after all this time, he had found someone like her just when he was about to get mated?

"Hey, Bash," called Julian, the only one who called by that name, "Why?"

"Oh. I met the most beautiful woman at the gym tonight. She was stunning."

As he spoke about this encounter, his face was bright and his eyes were shining. He was smiling as he spoke. "Wait, you don't think it could be the event planner lady?" asked Julian.

"Maybe, red hair, deep hazel eyes and curvy hips with the nicest set of breasts I've ever seen."

"I don't know about the breasts, she had a suit on when I met her, but she definitely had red hair and hazel eyes."

"The mating ceremony planner, really?"

Sebastian noticed Julian's surprised expression. He had to admit that only yesterday, he was angry that he had to mate with a total stranger, now he was glowing with interest for a woman he had just met hours ago.

"Bash," Julian called to him, but he didn't get a response. "Sebastian," he called a bit louder, "look at me."

Sebastian felt his brother grabbing his arm and turning him to face him. He had been lost in thought. "What?"

"You're getting mated in a little over a month."

"So? I get it. Okay."

"Sure."

They didn't talk any more about the event planner. They went over the investments of the day and reviewed the Los Angeles and Boston companies' mid-year results. They were very happy with the numbers.

Back in the kitchen, Elena finished her drink. She rinsed her cup and put it on the dish rack. Back in her room, she changed into her pajamas, which consisted of a pair of boy shorts and a camisole, then climbed into bed with her laptop. She reviewed the mating ceremony protocol for probably the hundredth time. She read the requests from the mate-to-be and her family, then the requirements from the king. After spending a half hour going over everything she closed the laptop. Elena was restless and edgy; she needed to expend some of this energy somehow. "Maybe I should go back to the gym," she said out loud.

She hesitated because she wasn't sure she wanted to see Bash again—her previous experience with him was rather overwhelming. Elena rubbed her hand over her face. She was frustrated about the unexpected attraction she had for this vampire. She needed to clear her head. She had never had much time for romance. Her life had always been busy with work and taking care of her family. Her only good times away from work and family were with James. She thought about him now and the good sex they shared.

She decided to try to find a good movie on TV instead, so she picked up the remote control from the nightstand and searched through the channels until she settled on an old war movie. She got comfortable in bed, shut the light off and lay back to watch the movie.

In the rest of the house, everyone was up and having a good time— some of them were playing video games or pool, while most of them were enjoying good drink and conversation. Sebastian was sitting on the large sofa with his future wife next to him. They were conversing with a group of people sitting around them.

"Where's Julian?" asked Klara.

"He's on a job for me."

"Oh," she said.

Everyone continued talking, keeping the atmosphere in the room pleasant and amicable. Sebastian was half listening to what everyone around him was saying while his mind was back with Elena at the gym. He thought about her skill with hand-to-hand combat, her body moving around him with such grace. He wondered why she wasn't down here with them. He wondered if Julian had invited her to join them.

"Sebastian," he heard his name.

"I'm sorry, yes?" he said.

"I was wondering if you've met the mating ceremony planner yet?" asked Klara.

"No, not yet. Julian is in charge of the plans."

"Oh, I'll ask Julian then."

After several hours, the rooms started to empty out as couples moved toward their rooms, while the single people took off to find someone for the night. Klara excused herself and left the room. After a while, Sebastian was left alone with one of his guards until Julian walked in the room.

"Any news?" asked Sebastian.

"No. I just finished a conference call with my informant. He's going to make some more inquiries then call us."

"Good. Hey, did you invite Elena to join us?"

"No, I didn't."

"Oh, remember to ask her tomorrow."

"Okay, I will. Well, I'm off. I'm going out for a couple of hours."

"See you later."

On his way to his room, Sebastian heard sobs coming from one of the rooms. He stopped for a moment, but decided to ignore it. As he began to walk away, he heard the sobs again, a bit louder this time. He moved in front of the door and turned the doorknob, opening the door slowly. From the soft light of the hall he could see that it was Elena.

His heart skipped a beat when he saw her lying there scantily dressed in her pajamas with no sheet on her. The sheet had slipped to the floor. He could sense the stress in her sobs. He was attempting to move closer to the bed when she jumped out of bed, flipped him on his back and held a knife against his throat.

"Elena," he said.

When Elena recognized his voice, she immediately pulled the knife away from his throat and sat on the floor next to him breathing heavily. "What the hell are you doing in my room?" she asked between breaths.

"Sorry," he said as he sat up next to her.

He looked at her tear-stained face and brought his finger to her cheek and wiped away her tears. "I heard sobs. I was concerned."

"Oh, I'm fine. Just nightmares."

"You want to talk about it?"

"No."

Their bodies were so close that their shoulders were touching. He could smell her delicious scent again. He could feel the immense heat growing between them. Sebastian slowly dipped his head and captured her lips with his. He nipped her lower lip, pulling at it softly. Elena opened up for him and quickly he thrust his tongue into her mouth. He put his hand on her waist and pulled her closer. As soon as he felt their bodies touch, Elena jumped out of his arms. She swiftly stood up and turned on the lamp on the nightstand. Sebastian pulled himself up from the floor and took a step towards her, Elena moved back.

"Don't."

"Why not?"

"I'm here to do a job, nothing else. I can't get involved with anyone," she said in a shaky voice.

"Fine," he said in a displeased tone. "I'll see you tomorrow at the gym."

"Yes sure, the gym."

Sebastian took a step away from her then turned around and walked out of the room closing the door behind him. He walked slowly down the hall, his body on fire again. He shifted his hard cock with his hand and kept walking. Her kiss was devastatingly delicious and he couldn't forget the taste of her in his mouth. One of the most intriguing things about her was her scent. Her vampire's blood had a mysterious, flowery note he had never encountered before.

Sebastian went straight back to his room and took a shower. His body was charged with so much energy that his cock was hard as a rock. The cold water was taking away some of the prickly feeling in his body. He poured shower gel into his hand, grabbed his cock squeezing the head hard then stroking from tip to base with hard and fast strokes. He continued with this motion, imagining Elena was under him while he thrust deep inside her. He stroked harder and faster and in a matter of minutes, he roared in relief.

Sebastian went to bed and continued to think about Elena. He smiled knowing there was more to come between them. He knew that as sure as he knew that she was his mate. He fell asleep thinking about her and the kiss they had shared.

CHAPTER THREE

ELENA WOKE UP TENSE. The stress of this assignment was getting to her. She knew it could very well get her killed, but getting her family to safety before she ended up dead was all that mattered. She sat on the edge of the bed for a few minutes before going to the bathroom to brush her teeth. She got dressed in her workout clothes.

Before she left, she checked her phone for an email or text from her sister then left for the gym. When she opened the door, she saw that Bash was already there. She walked over to him.

He seemed to sense her presence and turned around as she walked towards him. Her heart skipped a beat when he gave her a big smile. "Hi," he said.

"Hi," she said back.

"I'm just about ready."

"Give me a few minutes. Let me do some stretching first, okay?"

"Okay."

After they both slowly stretched their muscles, they faced each other and danced around slowly, moving tentatively. Suddenly he moved fast towards her so she veered to her left and sidestepped his attack. He turned swiftly to his back and elbowed her in the ribs. He twisted hard to the right and flipped her down on the mat. She quickly flipped back up to her feet.

They continued attacking and evading each other for more than an hour. The match ended when Sebastian took her by the shoulders and flipped her over on her face, ending up on top of her back.

Elena sharply took in a breath. She could feel every inch of his muscles stretched on top of her and also felt his huge erection. He didn't move from her back but shifted some of his weight off her by holding his upper body with his forearms. He could feel her body on fire underneath him.

He brushed her ponytail to the side with his hand and softly kissed her shoulder blade. Elena dropped her head to the side on the mat breathing hard. Sebastian rubbed his lower body against her ass cheeks causing a loud moan to escape from her lips. She wiggled her hips closer to his erection. He squeezed her lower stomach, an action that brought Elena to reality.

She suddenly tensed her body, causing him to pull his hand out and he sat down on the mat beside her. She rolled over on her back, breathing heavily just like he was. He reached for one of her hands and brought it to his lips. "You are amazing," he said.

Elena said nothing as she pulled her hand away and stood up from the mat. She didn't know what to do with all these sensations running through her body. She had never experienced anything like this before— even her erotic experiences with James hadn't brought these sensations. "I have to go. I'm meeting with Julian."

"Tomorrow?" he asked.

"Yes," she said walking away from him and out of the gym.

Elena showered and dressed. She looked herself over in the mirror, loving the feel of the fitted suit on her body. She enjoyed looking professional; it gave her the security she needed to dispel the nervous butterflies that fluttered in her stomach every time she thought about this job.

She shook her head, grabbed her carry case with her laptop in it, took one more look at her phone and then walked out of the room. She walked down the stairs, straight to the king's office and softly knocked on the door.

"Come in," she heard a man's voice say from within the room.

Elena opened the door and walked into the room. She found Julian and a woman sitting across from each other in a very nice sitting area. She walked over to them as Julian stood up and stood next to her.

"Hi Elena, this is Ms. Klara Gibbins," he said, gesturing toward the woman.

"Hi, I've heard a lot of great things about you," said Klara, shaking her hand.

"Thank you," she replied.

"Please sit," said Julian indicating the empty spot on the sofa next to Klara.

Elena sat down next to her and they launched into a conversation about the mating ceremony. She pulled out her laptop and went over the presentation of what she believed would be best. They had been meeting for more than an hour when Julian checked his watch, "Oh my, we've been at this too long. Let's take a break. Elena will update us by tomorrow, right?"

"Yes, definitely."

Elena put her laptop away inside the carry case. They all stood up at the same time, walked out of the room and said their goodbyes. Elena was feeling jumpy again. She walked up to her room, changed into her comfy jeans and a t-shirt and made her way back downstairs. She went out the same door she had the day before and walked out to the terrace and on into the garden. She walked further from the house this time, closer to the woods. The peace and quiet gave her the time to think carefully about the job at hand.

She found a small grassy area under a large tree and leaned into it. She pulled her phone out to check for messages. There was a text from her sister that she read and replied to. Then she pulled out her other phone and checked for messages from her leader. She saw that there was a voicemail message from him. She could hear the threat in his tone. After she finished listening she deleted the message.

She put both phones away and stood there for a few minutes. She spotted a narrow path into the woods, and since she needed solitude and to be close to the earth, she followed the path into the woods. When she felt she was far enough from the mansion, she kneeled on a clear patch of dirt, pushed her hands under and sifted it through her fingers. Feeling one with nature was one of her biggest thrills.

Sebastian searched every inch of the mansion looking for her. He asked everyone if they knew where she was. He rushed to the study and opened the door without knocking. Julian was sitting behind his desk on the telephone. Sebastian dropped with a heavy thump into the chair across from the desk. Julian kept talking on the phone but never took his eyes away from his big brother's serious, fuming face.

Julian hung up the phone and looked at him. Sebastian was in deep thought and didn't notice that Julian wasn't on the phone any longer. "What's up?" Julian asked.

"No one knows where Elena is," Sebastian shouted angrily.

"Really? Klara and I met with her earlier tonight."

"Did she said anything about where she was going after?" he asked.

"No, she didn't."

"Where can she possibly be?" he said out loud to no one in particular.

They sat there for several minutes, neither of them speaking, until a knock at the door broke the silence. "Come in," said Julian.

One of the guards walked in, he looked at Julian then Sebastian. "What?" asked Sebastian.

"My lord. She was detected by one of the garden cameras."

"And?" snapped Sebastian with a deep exasperated tone at how slowly the guard offered the information.

"She left the garden and walked into the woods. She's been gone for two hours. We don't have any video of her coming back."

"What?" Sebastian said jumping out of the chair and running at vampire speed out of the house with Julian and the guard behind him.

"Which way?" asked Sebastian slowing down.

"This way," said the guard running into the woods.

After miles of running through the woods looking for her, they finally found her. Elena was lying sideways on the ground with her head buried on her chest. One of her hands was half buried in the dirt. Sebastian stopped running and slowly approached her, signaling for the others to stay back. He moved quietly around the area then kneeled down next to her.

Softly he whispered her name, "Elena." She didn't respond. "Elena," he called again, a little louder this time.

He watched as she batted her eyelids a couple of times before opening her eyes completely. She looked at him and smiled, pulling herself up to a sitting position. Sebastian pulled her close for a hug and she wrapped her arms around him. "What's wrong?" she asked pulling away from him.

The other two were next to them by now. "You've been gone for hours," he commented still keeping her close to him.

"Oh, I'm sorry. I like being around nature. I didn't mean to worry anyone."

"That's fine, but I don't think you should be alone out here. There are wild animals in these woods. No more trips alone, okay?"

Sebastian could tell that Elena didn't like to be told what to do. She stared at the ground silently.

"Elena," Sebastian said in a sharper tone, pulling her face up to his.

"Fine," she snapped at him.

Both Julian and the guard looked at her but neither dared say anything. Sebastian grabbed her arms and pulled her up with him as he stood up. She pulled her arms away from him and took two steps back. Sebastian brought his hand to her face and cleaned some of the dirt from it. She didn't move, but as he caressed her chin, she leaned into his touch.

"Ah-hem," Julian cleared his throat.

They both looked at him. Sebastian took her hand and started to walk out of the woods. The other two vampires followed them closely.

"Did you feed tonight?" he asked her while they walked.

"No. I'm fine."

"You're sure?"

"Yes."

Sebastian felt her electrifying energy pouring into him. He could see the goose bumps on her arm. "You're cold," he observed, even though vampires are impervious to the cold.

"No, it's just..." she hesitated to finish the sentence, "I'm fine," she said drily.

When they reached the edge of the garden, Elena untangled her fingers from his and moved away from him. Sebastian stopped to address the guard who had stopped just short of the terrace. "Frank, thanks for everything."

"Okay," Frank said turning around and walking back to the front of the house.

Julian, Sebastian, and Elena walked into the house. She went through to the foyer then started up the stairs. "Elena, we need to talk," Sebastian called to her.

She turned around at the third step, putting a hand to her hips, "Listen, back off, okay? I already said I was sorry," she snapped at him then turned and continued walking up the stairs.

Sebastian watched her go up, staring at her back. Julian was about to go after her when Sebastian stopped him. He looked at his older brother with a grimace on his face. "What the hell?" Julian barked facing his brother. "She shouldn't be able to talk to you like that!"

"It's okay," Sebastian responded in a soft tone as he took Julian's arm and pulled him towards the study. When they were inside the room, Julian turned and gave him a serious stare, "What is going on, brother?"

"She doesn't know who I am."

"What? You're kidding me?"

"No," said Sebastian walking behind the desk towards the large window facing the gardens. As he looked out the window, he brought a hand through his hair, then turned to face his little brother.

"How is that possible?" asked Julian.

"I don't believe her boss ever showed her a picture of me. She must think that you're the king."

"Wow, crazy. So, tell her."

He turned back to look out the window, "No, I want her," he simply stated.

"That's never stopped you from telling any woman that you're the king."

He turned back to his brother, "Julian, she's the mating ceremony planner."

"Right. What are you going to do?"

"I don't know, but I never felt so connected to anyone as I do to her."

"So, get over it and fuck her. Your mating is in two months."

Sebastian rushed up to him and slammed him against the wall, pressing his forearm on his chest.

"Don't you ever talk about her like that," he roared.

Julian stared at him. In seconds, both vampires had their fangs out ready for a fight. Their eyes turned a deep red as they stared each other down. Julian retracted his fangs and raised his arms in the air as a sign of surrender. Sebastian backed up from him, retracting his fangs too, and his eyes turned back to their normal color.

"Got it?" he asked, still facing Julian.

"Got it," said Julian, "I think we both need a drink," he said as he moved behind the bar and poured two drinks.

He brought the drink to his older brother and they sat down on the chairs in front of the desk. They drank in silence, both very much in deep thought.

"Well let's get to work. There are a couple of conference calls scheduled for tonight," said Julian. He moved behind the desk and started the computer to look over what they had scheduled. They still had an hour before the first call, so he opened a report from his informant and together they discussed the matter.

Back in her room, Elena was already in the shower. She was troubled at her reaction to Bash. She bent her head forward and let the water run down her neck. She couldn't believe she was so rude to him. Her nerves were getting the better of her. Her unstable reaction when he got close was unsettling. Her body was throwing off so many pheromones that it was keeping her off balance.

She was here for one purpose and one purpose only, to assassinate the king and hopefully, in the process, keep her family safe. Bash was a distraction she wasn't prepared for. Every time his hard body was next to hers an exhilarating sensation ran through her like thousands of tiny needles pricking her everywhere.

Elena shook her head to clear out all this nonsense. She dried off and wrapped the robe around her. She pulled the laptop from the carry case and got comfortable on the bed. She opened the program she had designed specifically for this event and started working on the updates from the meeting.

She could feel the warmth of the sun through the open window. She didn't realize how long she had been working on this project. Satisfied that everything was completed, she saved the changes, closed the program and shut down the laptop. She opened the door and walked out on the small balcony. She smiled looking at the beautiful yellows and oranges in front of her as the sun started peeking out from the horizon. She closed her eyes as the sun's rays gently touched her face. She was so happy that being half Fae allowed her to feel the sun early in the morning and during the day, as long as she didn't stay out too long.

She yawned, covering her mouth. Her body was telling her it was time to sleep. She went back into the room, shut the curtains and climbed into bed.

CHAPTER FOUR

ELENA ABRUPTLY SAT UP in bed from a deep sleep. The nightmare she had was awful. She ran her hand over her face, wiping away the strands of hair that were plastered to her sweaty face. She rubbed her neck, feeling the hard knot that had settled there. She rubbed until she could no longer feel the tightness.

She was definitely ready for some exercise. She got dressed and walked out of her room. As she walked down the hall everything was quiet. She entered the gym, but this time there was no Bash. She started with her stretches, and as she began her workout, she saw him come in.

She stared at his body while he slowly moved toward her. He had no shirt on so she had the luxury of letting her eyes travel over his hard and broad chest and down to his abdominals, which were completely ripped and very flat. She didn't take her eyes away from him, blatantly admired every inch.

Bash stood in front of her, looking like the kind of man who was used to having women ogle him—and offer themselves to him. "If you keep looking at me like that, I'm going to start charging you," he said with a huge smile on his face.

"Really? How much?" she asked with a smile, tilting her head and looking up at him.

He took two steps closer to her, "I think a kiss would do," he said bringing his lips down to hers and delicately tasting them.

Elena leaned into his body as she nibbled on his lower lip. He moaned his approval then nipped at her to get her to open up. She opened her lips and he darted his tongue into her mouth.

He pulled her tight to his body. She fit perfectly between his thighs. Elena held onto his biceps tightly as she rubbed her body against his. They kissed for a long while, their tongues intertwining as they savored every bit of each other's mouths.

Elena's senses were overruling her mind. Not one thought as to why she should stop the kissing was coming through her mind. Then she saw an image of her little sister in her head, her small beautiful face smiling at her. That image brought Elena back to reality. She brusquely pulled away from him.

She took two more steps back as she tried to bring her breathing under control. Her body was full of too many sensations. Gasping for air, she said, "I don't how you do it, but when you're near me, I forget everything."

"Me too, baby," he said between breaths.

She looked into his beautiful blue eyes, "I'll give you a few minutes to stretch," she said.

"Thanks."

He stretched for a couple of minutes and then they sparred. She kept sharp because he was watching her intently—she kept her moves precise and deliberate, ready for anything he might throw at her. He tried to surprise her a couple of times, but she was able to repel his attack every time.

After close to an hour, he stopped sparring and stepped away from her, "You're very good," he said. "How about weapons?" he asked.

"Thanks, I'm good with a knife."

"I remember."

"I'm also a very good shot, but I prefer a knife."

He walked to a refrigerator against the wall and pulled out two bottles of water. He walked back and gave her one. She took the bottle and they both settled down on the mat. He brought his hand to her neck and gently caressed her collarbone with his thumb.

Elena loved his touch. She moved her head back slightly, opening her throat to him. He kept touching her but then lowered his head and softly kissed her neck. A moan escaped from her mouth. Elena turned her face toward his. She murmured something but he didn't seem to hear her. "Don't," she murmured a little louder this time.

Bash stopped what he was doing and continued with their conversation. "Where did you train?" he asked.

"On the streets with a friend. Being a young vampire with no protection, you learn how to defend yourself pretty quickly," she said.

"You have the protection of your leader," he stated.

"You don't know much about Levy. If you're not in his social clique, you don't exist," she said sarcastically.

"Impossible," he said. "According to reports to the king his pack is well taken care of."

"You should tell your king not to believe everything he reads."

"I have to go. I'm meeting about the wedding," she said as she turned and walked away from him. He stood up and moved quickly towards her. He grabbed her arm and turned her to face him. "Wait, let's get together after your meeting," he said.

"No," she said dryly. "I...," she hesitated. "I'm very busy with all the arrangements," she said not looking at him.

Sebastian took a deep breath before he calmly spoke to her as he let go of her arm. "Okay, see you tomorrow."

"Yes," she said quickly moving away from him and out the door.

Sebastian didn't want to believe her about Levy. He considered himself a fair and just king and by all accounts the European pack was doing great and everyone was happy, but she was telling a different story. He was also very exasperated with her. Her changes of mood were giving him whiplash. His body was vibrating with excess energy that had nowhere to go. When he looked into her beautiful hazel eyes, he genuinely wanted her to want him. Sebastian found a pair of gloves, put them on and started to take his frustration out on the punching bag.

Elena didn't know how she made it to her room. She had been tempted to turn back and go to him but she knew what the consequences would be. If she gave into her desires, the price would be too high. She reminded herself of the job at hand. She couldn't let the distraction of taking a lover put her family in jeopardy. She showered and put on another one of her nice suits. She combed her hair and wound it into a bun. She looked at the clock and saw that she had plenty of time left before the meeting, so she grabbed the phone on the nightstand and checked for messages. There were none, so she closed her phone and put it inside her blazer pocket.

She pulled her laptop out of the carry case and quickly checked her emails. After spending half an hour on the computer, she shut it down and put it back in the case. She picked up the case and walked out of the room. She ignored several people she passed in the hall. Just as she made it to the bottom of the stairs and stepped into the foyer, she saw Julian talking with a group of people. She moved swiftly away from the group and went out to the terrace.

She sat on a chair in the dark corner farthest away from the door. She closed her eyes and rested her head on the back of the chair. She couldn't get him out of her head: his body touching hers as they trained, the reaction of her body from his remarkable kisses. As she sat there with her eyes still closed, she could sense him near her. She opened her eyes and there he was sitting next to her. "Hi," he said.

"Hi," she said turning to him.

He took her hand and pulled her onto his lap. "How was your meeting?" he asked.

"No meeting yet," she answered.

"Good," he said as he brought his lips down to hers for a kiss. She wrapped her arms around his neck. With their tongues intertwined they kissed for a while. She could feel her body heating up. They continued kissing until she heard the terrace door open. She pulled away from him, waiting for someone to come out but nobody did. She stood up and straightened her suit. "I should go," she said.

"Yes," he merely replied.

She grabbed her carry case from the floor and walked away from him into the house. She moved fast through the living room where she saw several people had already gathered, then down the hall. She knocked on the door and waited for Julian to respond. "Come in," he said.

Elena opened the door and walked into the room. She sat down in the empty chair next to Klara. She pulled the laptop from her bag and started it up. She showed them several of the designs for the decorations according to their new specifications, along with their changes in the seating diagram and the new design for the vows ceremony. After they had gone over these items, Julian got up from his chair and walked to the bar. "Something to drink?" he asked her.

"No thanks," she answered.

He walked back with drinks for Klara and himself. They resumed their discussion of the plans. Klara requested several small changes to the dinner menu and they renewed their discussion of the music. After another hour, they agreed to meet one more time before Elena started to implement the plans. She shut down her laptop, put it in her bag and said her goodbyes.

Outside on the terrace, Sebastian had been silently sitting the whole time. He tried to wrap his head around her. What made her tick? What was keeping her from submitting to their desires? Nothing in his vast experience with women had prepared him for the battle raging within him—the battle with his desire for Elena.

He thought about what she had said about her leader. He intended to bring that up in his next meeting with Julian. He checked his watch and saw that it was past three in the morning. Julian should be done meeting with Elena. He stood up and walked into the house.

As he walked through the living room, he was greeted by a group of people who were sitting around talking. He continued on into the foyer where he was stopped by the head of his security team, who informed him that the changes to the security system were complete.

He walked down the hall to the study. The door was open, and as he walked in he saw Julian and Klara sitting on the sofa chatting quite intimately. He walked to the bar and grabbed a drink before sitting down in a chair in front of the couple.

"Hi Klara," he said.

"Hello Sebastian," she replied.

"How's everything going with the ceremony?" he asked.

"Good, actually great. The planner is fantastic. She's on top of everything."

"Yes, definitely. She's a wiz on her laptop," said Julian.

"Great. I have some things to go over with Julian," he said.

"Of course. I'll leave you two alone." said Klara evenly as she stood up from the sofa and walked out of the room. Julian's eyes followed her as she left. When she had closed the door behind her, he turned to face Sebastian. "What's up?" Julian asked.

"Do you have any reports from the European pack regarding misconduct or neglect to any members?"

"No. All the reports are satisfactory. Why?"

"Something Elena told me. She sounded resentful, even angry. Can you get a team in Europe and do some discreet investigating? Maybe some inquiries among the working class?"

"What do you expect to find out?"

"I'm not sure. Let me know what you do find."

"Okay."

Back in her room, Elena was on edge. Her head was throbbing with all the thinking she'd been doing this past week. She needed to go out. She changed into casual clothes and grabbed a small wallet from the drawer. She put her license and some money in it then grabbed her phone. She took a shoulder bag from the closet and put her wallet and laptop in it and grabbed her leather jacket. She moved quickly along the hall, down the stairs and out of the mansion. She walked to the garage and found a hot, slick motorcycle—every vampire had at least one. She got on and drove off.

Sebastian and Julian had finished the discussion on the European pack. "Have you fed yet?" asked Sebastian.

"No. You want to go together?"

"Sure."

They walked out of the study together and went into the living room. There they found several pack members chatting and laughing. They all turned and greeted the two men. Julian approached one of his guards, "Jacob, get us two donors. Bring them up."

"Okay," Jacob replied eagerly as he walked out of the room.

He and Julian sat and joined the conversation. After several minutes one of the guards walked in the room and quickly moved toward Sebastian. "Sire, may I speak to you for a moment?" he asked.

"Sure Chris," he replied, standing up and walking out of the room with him. Julian joined them as they stopped in the foyer. "What's up?" he asked.

"I'm about to find out," answered Sebastian.

The guard looked at both of them. "The ceremony planner left the mansion," he said.

"What?" they both replied together.

"I hope that's okay. I mean everyone is free to come and go, right?"

"Absolutely," Sebastian replied. "How long ago did she leave?" he asked.

"About thirty minutes ago," the guard answered.

"Damn it," snapped Sebastian.

"What the hell?" Julian asked.

"Thanks, Chris," said Sebastian.

The guard left them standing in the foyer and walked out of the house. He was furious; she was new to the area and she could get hurt. The vampire pack had many enemies. "We have to look for her," he stated.

"Where brother?" asked Julian.

"I don't know. Shit!"

"I'll ask the team doing the rounds in town to be on the lookout for her, okay?"

"Fine," he snapped.

He knew that Julian was right. There was no way to know which road she took; she could be in either one of the two towns in the area. Besides, they wouldn't want to draw too much attention to themselves by questioning the local humans. He pushed his hand through his long thick hair with frustration. He asked himself desperately where she could be going.

Julian tapped him on his shoulder. "Hey, let's feed," he said.

"No, you go," he said impatiently.

"Bash..." he started to say as Sebastian interjected.

"I'm fine."

"Okay, I'll make the call."

"Thanks little brother."

Julian walked down the hall to the study. Sebastian was suffocating—he needed some fresh air. He walked through the living room and out to the terrace. He found a quiet corner and sat down. After some time, Julian approached him. "We found her. She's in the diner at the truck stop off 171."

"Great. Do they know what she's doing there?"

"She's just working on her laptop. I'll be in my room if you need me."

"Go, I'll be fine," he said.

Julian turned around and started to walk away. "Julian," Sebastian called. Julian stopped and turned to look at his brother, "thanks."

"You're welcome."

Julian walked back into the house leaving his brother alone. Sebastian breathed in relief and leaned his head back on the chair. He closed his eyes, thinking about her. He was consumed with her. He sat there until he could see that the sun was rising.

He walked back into the house. Everyone was probably already seeking the shelter of their rooms and letting the daylight sleep take them. He didn't want to sleep. He sat on a sofa facing the foyer where he could see anyone that came in the house.

Elena had spent hours sitting in the corner booth in the busy truck stop working on her computer. She could feel the eyes of the other customers on her but no one had bothered her. She was past edgy now; every inch of her body was throbbing desperately. She had finished the work and now she was just staring at her open laptop. She knew that it was past dawn—the sun was high in the sky. She shut down her laptop and put it back in her bag.

Elena put on her jacket, pulled some money out of her wallet and left it on the table. She secured her bag over her shoulder and pulled her sunglasses out of the jacket pocket and put them on as she walked out of the diner.

CHAPTER FIVE

SEBASTIAN WATCHED ELENA WALK into the house. She walked slowly and looked like she was in some pain. She looked up and saw him standing in the living room doorway with his hand crossed over his chest. When she quickly headed for the stairs, he grabbed her arm. She tried to pull away but he had a strong hold on her.

"Bash, please," she gasped without looking at him.

Sebastian's face softened. "What's wrong?" he asked in a concerned tone.

"I don't know, I, I…" was all that came out.

"Look at me," he demanded sharply.

"I can't."

Sebastian moved in front of her. "Look at me," he insisted pulling her face up to his. He could see the need in her eyes, the same need he had for her. "Let me help you," he said now closer to her.

"How? My body…" was all she managed to say.

"I'll take care of you, darling," he said as he lifted her in his arms and quickly ascended the stairs.

Elena leaned her head on his chest and wrapped her arms around his neck. He walked straight to his room and approached the bed. He let her legs down, but held her tightly against his body. She was trembling all over, her face flushed. She was barely standing but he kept her from falling. He worked her bag and jacket off then sat her down at the edge of the bed.

He quietly removed her boots and socks. Elena leaned into him and brought her lips to his. Sebastian was slowly losing his control, the kiss bringing him closer to the edge. He fervently returned her kiss as he unbuttoned her blouse. He wanted her but this moment was for her. He needed to go slow and not scare her.

He pulled her blouse off then stopped kissing her. Softly he pushed her upper body on the bed and unbuttoned her jeans and slid the zipper down. "Babe, lift your bum for me," he spoke softly in her ear. Elena reacted quickly and lifted herself up. Sebastian rapidly removed her jeans then spread her legs and positioned himself between them.

"Bash," she whispered.

"Shush, I've got you," he said as he softly kissed her thigh, slowly moving up. He continued the trail of kisses up her leg until he reached her inner thigh close to her pussy. He moved the soft lacy material of her underwear out of the way and placed a kiss on her pussy, barely touching her. He didn't want to frighten her. Her body continued to tremble under him with his every touch and kiss.

Elena wiggled beneath him, pressing for more. Sebastian pulled her thong off, and as he dropped it on the floor, he admired the tattoo she had on her left pelvis. The design looked like wings and some sort of symbol. He softly rubbed the tattoo with his thumb.

"That's a nice tattoo. What does it mean?" he asked.

"Nothing," she quickly answered.

He could sense her hesitation to answer his question. He didn't want to upset her so he didn't reply and shifted his focus back to body. He opened her more, pulling her pussy lips apart. He slowly bent his head down and licked her from top to bottom, tasting her completely.

He decided not to pursue the issue of the tattoo. He held her hips down to keep her from moving, continuing to lick her until she squirmed. "Bash, oh my God, more, please," she pleaded with him, banging her fists on the bed.

"I will, babe," he said momentarily stopping.

He worked between licking and sucking her now. He could feel how much she wanted him. He sucked hard as he slowly inserted a finger inside her.

Elena just about jumped out of her skin when his finger went inside her. He watched her as she closed her eyes tightly, looking as her if body was on the verge of bursting.

Sebastian could feel the shift of her body. He thrust another finger inside her, shoving deeper. He pushed his fingers harder and faster as he took a tender nipple in his mouth and gave it a hard tug with his teeth. "Bash," she screamed as her body shattered under him, exploding into powerful tremors.

He persisted with sucking and thrusting inside her until the last of her tremors stopped, then her body collapsed beneath his touch in pure exhaustion.

He moved away, barely able to stand it. His cock was rock hard and pressing intensely against his jeans. He shifted his legs and with his hand repositioned his cock to give himself some relief.

He looked at her in the bed. She was looking at him with her eyes nearly closed. She was fighting sleep. He sat next to her in the bed and removed her bra. Gently lifting her, he shifted her body and slowly laid her head on the pillow. She made a soft sound. "Thank you," she managed to say as she shut her eyes.

Sebastian sat next to her for a few minutes, watching her take slow, soft breaths. He touched her face and gently pushed aside a few strands of loose hair. He covered her with the blankets and gave her a soft kiss on her lips. He found her intriguing.

He quietly moved off the bed and went to the bathroom. He couldn't stand his clothes any longer so he removed them and got into the shower. He let the cold water drift down his body. He was aroused to the limit, his hard cock pushing against his stomach. He found some shower gel, poured it into his hand and firmly grabbed his cock. He moved his hand up and down in a slow, precise motion. He continued this rhythm for a while and then sped up. He moved his hand harder and faster up and down, and with the other hand he squeezed hard on his sack. Relief blasted into his hand and he continued until there was nothing left. He moved under the water, washed himself, and got out. He pulled a towel and dried himself, wrapping the towel around his waist. He went to the other side of the bed, shut the light off, then removed the towel and climbed in next to her.

He wrapped an arm around her body and pulled her closer to him. She wriggled closer and fit her body tightly against his. The move exposed her neck to him. He could feel her blood running through her veins. His thirst for her blood was strong, his fangs elongating with the desire to taste her. He shook his head and retracted his fangs. He could wait; he knew she was his.

He closed his eyes and laid his head next to hers. He took a deep breath and inhaled her fascinating scent, memorizing it. He smiled as he fell into the deep sleep of the vampire.

Elena woke when he got into the bed as she tried to shift to her side but Sebastian's body was obstructing her. She turned over very stealthily and looked at him, then she slid away from him and slowly climbed out of bed. She moved away from the bed, looking around for her clothes.

"Elena," he called.

Elena stood at the end of the bed not saying anything, not even looking at him. He sat up enough to be able to see her. "Where are you going?" he asked.

"I, I, I should go," she answered.

"No you shouldn't. Come back to bed."

"Bash."

"Elena," he stated.

"I can't," she said picking up her clothes and moving to the door.

"I'll see you at the gym," he said.

"Maybe," she started to say.

"The gym, Elena," he said firmly.

Elena opened the door and walked out. Sebastian didn't go after her, but just watched her close the door. He collapsed back on the bed with a big smile on his face.

Elena quickly walked down the hall to her room. She stood naked against the closed door taking deep breaths. She moved to the bed and flopped herself on it with her legs dangling to the floor. She closed her eyes and ran her hand down to her lower stomach and into her pussy where she could still feel his mouth on her. In a million years, she never thought that it could feel so good. The guilt was eating her up. She couldn't believe that, with her family's safety in her hands, she could detour to experience one of the best orgasms ever. She shook her head. "I can't. What am I going to do?" she said out loud.

She moved to the bureau and pulled out some clean underwear and her gym clothes. She got dressed and put her hair back in a ponytail. She made it to the gym in no time, surprised at how quickly she moved.

When she opened the door, Bash was already there. She moved to the mat and started to stretch; Bash was doing the same. When they were both done with their stretches, they began to fight. They had been training against each other for about thirty minutes when Elena suddenly stopped. "I can't," she said stepping away from him.

"What?" he said reaching for her.

"No, don't," she said pulling from his reach.

Bash reached for her again, this time making sure to grab her hand. Elena sidestepped and flipped him onto the mat. He didn't let go of her hand, and with a swift move of his own, she landed flat on her back with him on top. "Bash," was the only thing that came out of her mouth before he engulfed her lips with his.

Elena opened for him and he thrust his tongue into her mouth. He pressed his whole body against hers, keeping some of the weight from her with his elbows. Elena could feel his hard erection on her stomach. She rubbed herself against it.

Bash moaned in her mouth as she rubbed her body on his. He kissed her for some time, slowly exploring her mouth with his tongue. She stroked his biceps, his shoulders and down his back. She moved underneath him. He pulled from the kiss and softly kissed a path down her throat. "Lift your arms, babe," he said.

Elena did as he asked and he pulled her sports bra off. He went back to kissing her throat then moved down to her breasts. He savored in between her cleavage as he moved one hand to cup her breast, gently massaging it and feeling the weight in his hand. It felt so good to touch her. He grabbed one of the hard peaks between his forefingers and thumb and lightly tugged and squeezed it.

Elena felt a throbbing energy down her core and between her legs. Her body reacted instantly to his touch. He moved his mouth to the other nipple, giving it equal attention. He twisted his tongue around it and gave a hard suck.

"Bash," she murmured. He loved his name in her mouth; her voice was pitched with so much need. He kneeled in front of her and pulled off her shorts and thong. He caressed under her breasts then her stomach as he tracked kisses downward. "Bash, please," she begged him with her eyes half-closed.

"Soon, babe. I want you so much."

He moved his mouth to her mound; she lifted up seeking his mouth. He pressed her down, holding her with his hands. She spread her legs wider accommodating his shoulders. He put his hands under her butt, worked his tongue up and down her, taking soft nips. He continued to nibble and suck her.

Elena couldn't hold out any longer. He was keeping her at the edge of climax. He stopped and moved away from her. She uttered her irritation when he moved his mouth from her, "Please don't stop."

"Soon," he said as he sat between her legs and pulled his sweatpants off. He brought his body on top of her as he took her mouth in a wild kiss. He caressed her face and neck as they continued kissing, tongues dancing and tasting each other.

He pulled away from her lips. "I want to be inside you," he whispered softly in her ear.

She felt as though her entire body was glowing with desire, her whole body quivering under him. She looked into his eyes, as her eyes shimmered with desire.

"Elena," he murmured between clenched teeth.

Elena didn't take her eyes from him. She could see the strain on his face. She moved her hand up to his face and caressed it, then gently traced his lips with the tip of her thumb. She gave him a big smile. "I need you," she said.

Sebastian smiled back to her as he positioned the tip of his cock at her entrance. He began to thrust his shaft inside her little by little. She was so ready for him. He moved tentatively as if he was trying not to hurt her.

Elena was on the verge of melting underneath him, the pressure of his cock inside her was sending tremendous shocks of pleasure through every part of her body. She tried to adjust her body to his prodigious size. He thrust some more until she felt him all the way inside her. "Babe, it's going to be okay."

All she could do was nod her head; her body wanted more. He seemed to sense what she wanted and thrust fast and hard inside her. She gave a deep groan as she dug her nails into his back. Sebastian didn't move, he caressed her face as she adjusted to him.

"Okay?" he asked still caressing her.

"Yes, please do something."

"Oh yes, darling."

He thrust in lengthy motions, taking his cock out almost to the crown then fully back inside her. She found his rhythm and moved her hips up to meet him. They moved in complete unison both finding the ultimate pleasure. She turned her head to the side, giving him a complete view of the throbbing vein in her neck. She could feel that his fangs were elongated as he lightly scraped them on her neck. "Mmmm, mmmm," was her only response.

He moved faster now, thrusting deeper and harder. Without asking her, he bit into her neck softly and drank from her. Her body exploded in a massive orgasm that rolled into multiple orgasms as he continued to feed from her.

Her body was in total ecstasy, quivering under him. She held tightly to him as, between her own orgasms, he burst with his own. After several minutes he stopped drinking, licked the puncture wounds closed and continued shoving hard inside her, not slowing down until both were completely satisfied and the tremors stopped.

He lifted his weight from her for a moment, then looked into her eyes. Could he see the uncertainty on her face? She hardened her expression so there was a sharp edge to her eyes. She felt too vulnerable, as if she would melt into his eyes if she let herself, so she made her face into an impregnable mask. He pulled out of her and moved to the side. He put his sweatpants on, walked over to a bench and grabbed a towel. While his back was turned she quickly sat up and put her sports bra on.

"Let me clean you," he said sitting in front of her.

"No, I've got it," she said taking the towel from him.

He sat back on the mat watching her as she cleaned herself. She put on her thong and shorts, looking everywhere but at him.

"Elena, look at me," he said pulling her face towards him. "We need to talk," he said keeping his eyes on her.

"Why?"

"Elena," he warned her.

"I have to go. I've got a meeting with Julian," she said as she stood up from the mat.

"Fine, later," he said standing next to her.

"I can't. I'm busy."

"Elena, I want to know you better."

Elena looked at him, she felt the sincerity in his words but she couldn't get close to anyone right now. So many questions crossed her mind: Why now? Why this? Why did he have to reach out to her so much?

Elena could sense his body tighten in displeasure as she remained silent. She was getting ready to fight him on this but she realized that he would have none of it.

"You're mine," he said grasping her arm, "Don't forget it," he said firmly then dropped his hand.

She didn't know what to say. She turned to leave but then turned back. "I'll be in my room after the meeting," was all she said turning around and walking out of the gym.

Elena walked directly to her room and took a long hot shower, trying to clear her head. She dressed in another of her suits and worked her hair into a bun. She picked up her phone and checked for messages. Her sister had sent her one so she read it right away then deleted it.

Elena checked her other phone where there was another nasty voice message from her leader. She listened to the entire message as her stomach turned into knots. She put the phone back in the top drawer, checked herself one last time in the mirror, then grabbed her carry case and walked out of the room.

CHAPTER SIX

ELENA TOOK HER TIME walking down the stairs, her mind going over and over the situation with this assignment and the slim possibility of her coming out of it alive. She had no hope for herself but she knew she could get her mother and sister through it alive. She moved slowly, stepping lazily. She got to the foyer, turned down the hall and walked to the study. She knocked on the door and waited. "Come in," Julian said. She opened the door and walked in. The two of them already had drinks in their hands. "Drink?" Julian asked.

"No, thanks."

She pulled her laptop out and all three jumped right into the ceremony plans. They worked for several hours until Julian and Klara agreed on the plans, with a few small changes requested by Julian. They reviewed the plans one last time. Elena shut off the computer and put it inside her case.

"Elena, you're doing a great job," said Klara.

"Thanks. I'll start making calls tomorrow."

"Great. Do you want to join us? We're getting together for a game of pool," said Julian.

"No, thanks."

"Are you sure?" asked Klara.

"Yes," she answered.

The three of them walked out of the room together. When they reached the foyer, Elena said goodbye to them and walked up the stairs.

When Julian and Klara reached the entertainment room it was already full of people playing video games and shuffleboard. The atmosphere was cheerful. Klara walked up to a group of women she knew while Julian joined the group at the billiard table.

Julian chatted with the guys while waiting for the current game to end. He took a beer that one of the men offered him and took a big sip of it. He looked up to check on Klara and found her looking at him too. They smiled at each other and went back to chatting.

Sebastian was in his office trying to complete some work but he couldn't concentrate on anything. Everything was a blur to him. He tapped furiously on the keyboard; he had managed to freeze his computer. Realizing that he was getting nowhere tonight, he got up and walked out of his office.

As he walked down the hall he could hear laughter coming out of the entertainment room. He walked in and said hello to the women first, then he moved around saying hello to the men.

He moved to the bar and grabbed a beer, then went to the billiard table and stood next to his brother who was in the middle of a shot. He watched the game and the players who were all chatting and laughing. Within five minutes, the match was over and Julian's team had won. The brothers stood next to each other drinking beer and watching two other groups play. "I have a report of a small incident I want to go over with you," said Julian discreetly.

"Okay," Sebastian said.

They walked out of the room and down the hall to Julian's office. Julian moved behind the desk as Sebastian sat down across from him. Julian started up his computer and together they perused the reports from the arresting guards regarding the incident. Sebastian knew both of the vampires; they were young and a bit rowdy, but good kids.

"As you can see, we already reprimanded them for their behavior," Julian said.

"Great. Anything else?"

"Yes, our IT team has discovered several illegal email messages from a hidden source regarding the alleged attempt on the your life. It's been going on for several days."

"So where is it coming from?"

"They don't know that yet. The team is working long hours trying to locate the origin of the messages."

"Really?"

"Our head of intelligence reports that the culprit is a highly intelligent person and probably an expert hacker. All the messages are being transmitted illegally at peak time."

"This is crazy," said Sebastian who was now pacing back and forth in front of the desk. "Is there anything we can do?" he asked stopping in front of Julian.

"Nothing, it's out of our hands. It's up to our IT people."

"Okay, keep me informed. Anything on Europe?"

"Net yet. So how did it go with Elena last night?"

"What? It went fine," he answered avoiding eye contact.

"Sebastian," Julian warned him.

"I've got this, okay?" he said firmly.

Julian threw his hands in the air, "Okay."

"I have to go," said Sebastian walking out the door.

Back in her room, Elena completed the few changes to the ceremony and made a checklist of the calls she needed to make tomorrow. She also checked her email for a message from her sister. "I hope this works, little sister," she said out loud.

Just as she was shutting off her laptop, she sensed Bash opening the door. She looked up from her sitting position in bed to see his face wearing a big smile. As she closed her laptop and put it inside the bag he walked over to her. She loved the way he moved and she noted how sexy he looked in a tight dark t-shirt and fitted low-rise black jeans.

"Hi," he said leaning over to her and capturing her lips between his own. He looked at her and said, "I love the way you look at me."

"Hi," she said back.

She moved to the side and made room for him to sit down on the bed. He kicked his shoes off and climbed in bed with her.

"You're so beautiful," he said caressing her face.

He pulled out the pins that held her bun up and spread her hair out with his fingers. She leaned into his touch. "I've wanted to do this since the first time I saw you," he said.

She didn't want to feel these emotions. She straightened herself and moved away from him. Apparently, he felt her shield go up and he seemed to change tactics. "How are the plans going?" he asked.

"Plans?"

"Ceremony plans," he specified.

"Oh, they're going great. We finalized the plans tonight. I'll start to make calls tomorrow."

"Good."

He reached for her again, but this time he slowly stroked her upper arms with his fingers. "What happened last night?" he asked.

"What do you mean?"

He continued touching her, "You went out, remember?"

"I didn't know I had to ask for permission?" she snapped.

He stopped moving his fingers, "Elena," he warned her.

"Fine, I felt caged in."

"Why?"

"I'm not sure. I didn't know what to do with myself. My body was craving something."

"Or someone?" he asked smiling at her and going back to caressing her arm.

Elena didn't know what to say to him. She closed her eyes and took a deep breath.

"Elena, look at me," he said in her ear.

Elena was startled by his closeness but she didn't move away, she craved that closeness. She was addicted to his touch already.

"Elena," he whispered as he tugged on her earlobe with his teeth. Elena opened her eyes as he moved his lips around her ear then down her chin. He stopped as he connected with her eyes. He smiled at her. She took a short breath in and smiled back at him. "Breathe, babe." She let go of her breath and continued smiling. "Now say it. You craved me," he said stroking her chin with his thumb.

"Yes," she purred into his touch.

Sebastian seized her lips, savoring them with his tongue while softly tugging and nipping with his teeth. Elena leaned closer to him and opened up for him. He moved his hands to her waist and lifted her onto his lap.

Elena wrapped her arms around his neck as she offered her open mouth to him. He seized her tongue. Their tongues mingled together in an earth-shaking kiss that lasted several minutes. She didn't want him to stop but they needed to come up for air. They both were breathing heavily. Her lips were red and swollen from his kisses.

He dipped his head and worked his mouth down her neck in gradual tentative motions, tasting every inch of her throat. Elena closed her eyes and dropped her head back enjoying the feeling of his mouth on her. "Babe, lift your arms for me," he said between kisses.

Elena did as he asked and swiftly he pulled her camisole off and threw it on the floor. Her pussy was throbbing. She wiggled her butt into his erection, rubbing against it, looking for any way to relieve the intense pressure between her legs.

Sebastian grabbed her hips and changed the angle of her body. She was now straddling him, giving him better access to her pussy, and slowly he rubbed the entire length of his erection while he sucked one of her nipples. She groaned softly as a boost of electricity ran through her whole body and back to her pussy. "Bash, please. I want to come," she purred.

"Soon, babe."

He switched to the other nipple while letting go of her hips and taking the other nipple between his forefinger and thumb. She continued rubbing herself on him, barely keeping herself up by holding onto his arms. She couldn't hold the noise inside any more, now she was moaning and groaning out loud as the pressure in her pussy escalated.

Sebastian took a nipple deep in his mouth, sucking hard, and he pinched the other one with his fingers. Elena's head dropped back. She screamed out loud as her body burst in a massive climax that shook her entire body. She held onto him, digging her nails into his upper arms. Her body quivered on his lap for several minutes. She leaned her head on his chest taking short hard breaths.

Sebastian brought her firmly against his chest and softly kissed the top of her head, gently stroking her back as the trembles slowed. After some time, she lifted her head and looked into his eyes. "That was incredible," she whispered between gasps for air.

He lifted her up from his lap and laid her flat on her back on the bed. He took his t-shirt off then his jeans and briefs, leaving him naked in front of her. Elena's eyes brightened. She licked her lips and with a shaky hand reached for his cock.

Sebastian stood still as her hand stretched out toward him. Elena took his cock by the base with her hand. Slowly she moved her hand up to the tip as she grabbed the base with the other hand. She kept the touch gentle while she stroked her thumb on the tip and brought the other hand up his length, now slowly tightening her grip. She continued to slide her hands up and down his cock in a slow motion.

He took her hands from him, settled her back on the bed and fitted his body in between her legs, which she instantly spread for him.

Sebastian stroked his hands down her chest to her lower stomach. He moved his fingers down to her pussy, slipped them inside her, and pumped her fast and hard. He brought his lips to hers and sparked a frantic clash of tongues. He thrust his fingers deep inside her, where her juices were flowing. Her pussy drew his fingers in, holding them fast inside her.

When she started to tremble again, he removed his fingers and positioned his shaft at her entrance. "Babe, look at me," he said.

Elena lifted her eyes from his body and connected with his eyes. He smiled at her as he leisurely thrust his cock inside her. She wrapped her legs around his waist while caressing his long hair and gently kissing his chest. He pulled his cock out, barely leaving the tip in, and thrust deep inside her again.

She gasped loudly as her pussy was stretched to the maximum. She grasped his arms as her head fell back, lifting her breasts. He took a nipple in his mouth nipping and scraping with his teeth. Elena's head dipped farther back, opening her throat for him. His fangs elongated as he lifted her butt higher and thrust hard and deep. He dipped his head and bit down on her neck, hungrily swallowing her blood.

Elena screamed her relief as he bit down on her neck, her body combusting in tremble after tremble as Sebastian pumped faster and harder inside her. He stopped sucking her blood and licked the wounds while continuing to pump inside her.

"Babe, look at me," he murmured in her ear.

Elena opened her eyes and looked into his beautiful blue eyes. Sebastian moved his hair out of the way and offered his neck to her. Elena's eyes opened wider; she couldn't believe what he was doing. She couldn't think straight because her body was overriding her brain, but she knew the repercussions of taking his blood. She shook her head to him denying the offer. His eyes turned red instantly; she could sense his anger. Sebastian didn't stop but pumped faster and in seconds he blasted his cum inside her. He continued until the last of their trembles stopped.

Elena didn't know what she should do next. He was angry with her, she could see it in his face. Sebastian pulled out from her, walked into the bathroom, cleaned himself then went back to her with a wet cloth in his hand. Elena reached out to take the cloth from him.

"No, let me do it," he said sitting by her side and gently cleaning the juices of their pleasure.

"Why?" he asked.

"What?" she said, answering his question with another question.

"Elena," he warned her. "I offered you my blood," he said as he finished cleaning her.

Elena hesitated. She closed her eyes and pulled her face away from him. How could she explain to him that she would be dead within weeks and that she didn't have the time for a permanent relationship? A small tear rolled down her cheek and quickly she wiped it away.

"Elena, look at me," he demanded.

She moved away from him and lifted herself into a sitting position. She turned her head and looked at him. She put a strong and firm front up for him. She couldn't let him see her weakness.

"I'm here for only one purpose—to do a job—to plan a mating ceremony. That's it," she said with steel in her voice. She couldn't allow herself to care for him when her family was in danger for their lives. She had to stay focused.

He gave her a hard look, "What does that have to do with us?" he asked brusquely.

"There is no us. This is just sex," she stated.

"What? Don't try to diminish what we have together. This is more than sex and you know it," he snapped.

"I don't know anything. I want to be alone, please leave," she said as she climbed out of the bed and started to walk to the bathroom.

Sebastian rushed to her, grabbing her arm, and pulled her into his body. He wrapped his arms around her waist and slammed her body against the wall. "I see what you're trying to do," he snapped.

"I'm not trying to do anything," she snapped back at him.

"You're mine," he said lowering his head and forcefully crashing his lips into hers.

Elena tried to fight his hold but to no avail. Her body melted into his and she opened up for his kiss. He punished her mouth with a wild and ferocious kiss. He stopped abruptly and took a few steps away from her. She looked into his eyes. She moved away and walked into the bathroom and closed the door leaving him standing there. She could hear him pick up his clothes from the floor and quickly get dressed.

Elena was holding her breath leaning against the door. Her legs were shaking so much that they barely kept her up. She let go of her breath when she heard him slam the door behind him. She moved into the shower stall and turned on the water. She forced herself under the water as her tears began to fall. Her heart ached; she knew it was a mistake to get involved with him but she had never felt like this before. This was all so new to her. She needed to finish this job and save her family, no matter what she felt for him.

She shook her head, determined to put this incident behind her. She quickly showered, dried herself off and put her robe on.

Sebastian walked into the entertainment room and went straight to the bar where he poured himself a shot of rum. He swallowed the shot fast and poured another one, which he swallowed just as fast.

"Wow, brother," said Julian.

Sebastian turned to him and gave him a hard look. He didn't flinch as he took a third shot.

"Who's got you so worked up?" Julian asked.

"No one," Sebastian answered slamming the glass on the bar then walking away from Julian and out of the room.

Julian followed Sebastian as he moved down the hall and into his office. Sebastian left the door open behind him. Instead of walking to his desk, Sebastian moved to the sitting area and sat in the corner chair. Julian followed him and sat across from him.

"What gives?" Julian asked.

Sebastian gave him another hard looked before he answered him, "I'm fine."

"Woman trouble? Maybe a gorgeous petite redhead?" queried Julian.

Sebastian glared at his brother, "What do we know about Elena?" he asked.

"What do you mean?"

"Any family, mother, father, you know?"

"Based on her file, she has no family. She worked in a large event-planning firm in Russia and part-time at a meat market owned by her best friend's father. She has a small apartment, lives alone."

Sebastian absorbed this information. He felt sad for her.

"You want me to have her investigated?" asked Julian.

"No," he answered suddenly. "Is there anything we need to go over?" he asked, changing the conversation.

Julian watched him for a moment then spoke, "Yes, I have it on my computer."

"Okay, let's go to your office," he said standing up and walking towards the door.

"Sure."

CHAPTER SEVEN

ELENA WOKE UP EXHAUSTED. She had nightmare after nightmare about Arnav and her mother and sister. On top of all that, her body was craving Bash's touch. She turned around on her bed and looked outside. The sun was still shining, but she couldn't stay in bed any longer.

She put on her heavier workout clothes and grabbed her socks and sneakers and put them on. She pulled one of her small knives from the nightstand drawer and inserted one in her sock and pulled her pant leg over it. She knew she needed to get rid of the excess energy in her body.

She picked up her phone and put it in her pocket and walked out of her room. She pulled the hood over her head, and at vampire speed, moved to the stairs, through the living room and out of the house. She slowed when she got to the terrace and looked around for anyone before running into the woods.

When she was out of sight from the house, she slowed her pace and ran at a human jogging speed. She decided to take the same path as before; the tall trees gave her some protection from the sun. She ran with no destination in mind, trying to flush some of the intense longing out of her body. This craving was a distraction she hadn't planned for.

She ran for some time until she could see that the path she was on was about to end. She saw a wide space between two groups of trees, left the path, and ran straight through the opening. She ran for what seemed forever until she saw how little of the sun's yellow rays were left in the sky. She knew it was time for her to turn around, so she did a quick u-turn and ran back the way she came, speeding up a bit now. In minutes she was back on the path. She kept the pace a bit faster than human speed and was soon back at the edge of the woods in sight of the garden. She stood there for a few minutes admiring the beauty of the garden.

Elena walked fast out of the woods and into the garden, then slowed down as she reached the terrace. She walked into the house and down the hall to the gym. The aching in her body was overwhelming, and her heart was beating faster now with the anticipation of seeing Sebastian.

Elena opened the door and walked in. She expected him to be there but he wasn't. She went to the punching bag, pulled her sweatshirt off and grabbed a pair of gloves. She moved in front of the punching bag and started punching, flipping the stand several times with punches and kicks. She continued for several minutes then froze for a moment when she sensed Bash walk in the room. She ignored his approach and went back to punching.

He stood behind her, moving closer. Elena stopped punching but didn't turn around to look at him. Sebastian pressed his body against hers. He wrapped an arm around her waist and pulled her tight. "Hi," he said kissing her bare shoulder.

"Hi."

"I see you started without me," he said close to her ear.

Elena didn't speak, she just leaned closer to him. She loved his male scent, the strength his body gave off. He moved away from her, walked to the wall and grabbed a pair of gloves. He came back over to her as he put the gloves on.

She turned around to face him. Slowly they moved in a circle, sizing each other up. Suddenly, he threw a punch that she was able to evade easily. He smiled at her as he threw a combination at her. This time she evaded one but not the other. The punch caught her on her shoulder, slamming her back a step. Quickly she moved back into position. She threw several combination punches at him with no significant impact.

They worked around each other, punching and parrying for some time. Elena was distracted for just a second by a drop of sweat she saw going down his chest to his stomach and into his sweatpants. At that moment he threw a punch that caught her on her jaw snapping her head back. She landed on her ass on the mat.

Bash ran to her. Kneeling in front of her, he pulled his gloves off and checked her face.

"Stop," she said slapping his hands away from her. "Do you attend to all your sparring partners when you hit them?" she snapped at him, still trying to remove his hands.

"No, because I've never sparred with my woman before," he said caressing the now purplish jaw.

She pulled her gloves off too. His touch initiated a charge through her body right down to her pussy. She could feel the arousal coming fast. She could tell that he sensed her state of arousal right away. "Bash," she murmured hardly able to talk.

He took her open mouth in a wild kiss encircling an arm around her back while pressing her down to the mat. She hung onto him by wrapping her arms around his neck not wanting to stop savoring his taste. He kissed her lips, then trailed kisses down her chin.

Bash lay partially on top of her, keeping a leg between hers. He moved his free hand down to her lower stomach softly slowly working his way between her sweatpants and underwear. He pushed her pussy lips apart and slid his finger down her entrance. He pressed down hard, circling but not entering her quite yet.

After a few seconds he pushed one finger inside her, pumping her fast. Elena wiggled her pelvis up as he inserted a second finger. Her body was aching for him. "Let me come," she slurred.

"Not this time, babe. I want to be inside you," he said as he pulled his fingers out.

He moved his leg off of her, pushed her sweatpants and underwear off then removed his own. He settled between her legs, softly caressing her legs with his hands. He brought his body on top of hers and positioned his shaft at her entrance. He lifted her legs up and gradually thrust inside her.

Elena loudly groaned with pleasure. He dipped his head down and continued voraciously kissing her throat. As he plunged deeper inside her, her body responded by tightening her pussy walls like a glove around his cock. His thrust became urgent from his need for her. He thrust faster and deeper pulling her legs up to his shoulders.

He slammed at her hard, then brought his hand between their bodies and, at the same time, he pinched her clit as he bit down with his fangs. Elena let loose in an immense orgasm that rolled into others as Sebastian continued to thrust inside her. Seconds after she came, he followed with his own orgasm blasting his cum inside her.

He continued until both bodies stopped shaking. He pulled from her and flipped onto his back bringing her with him. Elena laid her head on his chest trying to get her breath under control.

Bash pulled some loose strands of hair from her forehead as he gently drew soft circles on her lower back. She closed her eyes for a moment, relaxing in his embrace and enjoying his touch. Elena was glad he didn't ask her to take blood from him this time. She didn't want to fight with him. She brushed her fingers softly on his chest. "That was intense," she said.

"Yes," he said.

"I have to go. I have calls to make," she said sitting up next to him.

"Okay, I'll come to your room later."

"Maybe," she said as he interrupted her with a finger on her lips.

"Don't even try it. Be there."

She didn't look at him as she grabbed her clothes and got dressed.

"Elena," he warned her pulling her face to him. He held her chin forcing her to look straight into his eyes. "I'll meet you in your room," he repeated to her.

"Fine," she snapped at him.

Bash leaned in for a quick kiss then let go of her chin. She finished putting her clothes on and stood up. She could feel his eyes on her as she walked out of the gym.

In her room, Elena quickly showered and chose a short summery dress from the closet and put it on. She combed her hair and decided to braid it. She found her carry case and pulled her laptop out. She settled in the middle of the bed and made herself comfortable with pillows at her back. She started up the laptop and opened the list of companies she needed to call today. She grabbed her phone and dialed the first number.

As she completed one more call, her other phone rang. She pulled the phone from the drawer and saw the text message her sister sent her. She read the message then replied.

Elena put the phone back in the drawer. Confident that she completed the necessary calls, she closed the program and shut down the laptop. She climbed out of bed, put the laptop away then went into the closet and pulled a tablet from a small case hidden at the back.

She settled back on the bed and accessed the vampire private network. Elena knew that the only way to attract the vampire council's attention on the matter of the king's assassination was to invade the network. She keyed in several codes pulling down the firewall, then she entered several encrypted messages in the main frame of the vampire network. After several minutes of spreading the information onto several servers she signed out. She had been working the site for several days, inundating the system with the information that the king's life was in danger.

After Sebastian had worked for several hours with Julian in his office he was ready to leave. He shifted restlessly in his chair, and Julian could tell his brother was only half listening to what he was saying.

"Bash, Sebastian, man are you listening?" shouted Julian.

"What?" asked Sebastian snapping out of his dazed state.

"Really, bro. What's up with you?"

"Nothing, I'm fine. Are we done?"

"Yes," replied Julian.

Sebastian jumped out of his chair, "Then see you tomorrow," he said on his way out the door. Julian stared at the door shaking his head. As he was about to leave his office, the phone rang. "Hello," he said.

As he listened quietly to the other person on the phone, his face turned serious and the edges of his mouth became hard. When the man stopped talking, Julian screamed into the phone, "What is your team doing about it?"

"Julian, we are working diligently on this matter," replied the vampire at the other end of the phone.

"Not diligently enough! Your team is still no closer to knowing who the culprit is," he continued to scream.

"We are doing everything possible to find him."

"Fine, keep me updated on your progress," he yelled, banging the phone receiver onto the base.

"Damn it," he said out loud.

Julian moved from behind the desk and walked out of the room.

Sebastian made his way to Elena's room, having been stopped several times along the way by some of his pack members. As their king, he felt the need to have open and friendly discussion with them. He opened the door without knocking and walked into her room. He saw that the bed was empty and the bathroom door was open. He looked around but didn't see her.

He felt the breeze coming from the open balcony door. He walked to the door and stopped at the threshold. He saw her standing with her hands holding onto the railing. She was wearing a fitted short dress that barely covered her bottom.

Elena turned around as he crossed the threshold, their eyes met and she walked towards him. He opened his arms for her and she stepped into them. She molded herself into his body as he embraced her. She lifted her head and gently pulled his head down by the back of his neck and kissed him on the lips.

They continued kissing for some time. Elena lowered the hand on his neck and stroked his back as he grabbed her butt pressing her hard against his erection. He was pleased that she was so happy to see him. He was confident that tonight he would get her to drink from him.

She leaned into his erection as he continued to devour her mouth, twisting and battling with her tongue. He stopped kissing her and took her hand, leading her inside the room.

He stopped at the foot of the bed and pulled her straps down her shoulders and off her arms, then pulled the top of the dress down to her waist, baring her breasts. He lowered his head and dropped soft kisses around her breasts, alternating between them while kissing and licking them. He moved his mouth to a nipple and twirled around it with his tongue as he gently teased the other one between his fingers.

"Mmm, mmm," she moaned closing her eyes as her head dropped back.

Sebastian stopped for just long enough to say, "You love it when I suck your nipples, babe," he said.

"Yes, please don't stop," she whispered.

Sebastian went back to her nipple, sucking it deep and hard. Elena grabbed the back of his head and held him tight to her breast. He continued his assault on her breasts, taking turns with each one. He stopped and pulled away from her body.

"Bash," she complained.

He stood in front of her and took his clothes off. Elena watched him, her appreciation showing plainly on her face as her eyes drifted from the lean muscles on his stomach to his broad chest. She pushed her dress down her legs and kicked it aside, then pulled her thong off kicking that away too.

Sebastian lightly caressed her collarbone with the back of his hand, slowly moving down and circling her breasts then continuing to her stomach then to the top of her mound. With his knee, he nudged her legs open and brought his hand to her pussy, softly pressing the lips apart with his fingers. Elena put her hands on his shoulders trying to steady her body, which was already trembling with desire. He rubbed his fingers up and down her pussy pushing lightly inside her. He took a nipple in his mouth as he worked her pussy with his fingers.

Sebastian couldn't hold back his craving for her any longer; he wanted to be deep inside her. He removed his fingers from her, picked her up at her waist and flipped her onto the bed face down. He softly kissed her back while taking a hold of her hips and lifting her butt in the air. He spread her legs with his body and positioned himself between them. He took his cock in his hand and swiped the tip between her ass cheeks, then down her pussy, then back up. Her body trembled more.

"Bash, please," she murmured.

"Please what, babe? Tell me what you want."

"Bash."

"Ask me sweetie. Tell me to fuck you."

"Fuck me now, please."

Sebastian spread her legs wider and pressed his cock tip at her entrance and plunged deep inside her. He pulled back out as far as the tip then plunged deep inside again. He thrust in and out deeply for some time. He leaned forward and gently kissed her back again. He worked her pussy hard, thrusting deeper every time he went in. She was quivering frantically.

He moved closer between her legs, held her hips still and thrust faster, slamming hard on her butt. She couldn't wait any longer. "Bash," she screamed.

"Soon, babe."

Elena swung her hips back as he pushed into her. They continued moving together, slamming their bodies hard against each other. Sebastian picked up speed as he brought a hand to her pussy, finding her clit and pinching it hard between his fingers.

Elena screamed out as her orgasm exploded, bringing with it a cascade of shivers. He continued pumping into her, then brought his fangs to her neck. Biting down hard, he drank her blood. Elena's body erupted into another huge orgasm as Sebastian exploded inside her with his own climax. He slowed down the thrusts but continued with short ones for several minutes until they both stopped shaking, then he collapsed on the bed. Sebastian slid to her side onto the bed and wrapped an arm around her. He looked into her eyes and saw they were dazed with ecstasy.

He pulled his hair aside and offered his throat for her to feed as he did the previous night. Her eyes closed but not quickly enough for him not to see the panic inside them. She shook her head and burrowed it into his chest, hiding her face.

"I can't," she murmured.

"Elena."

"I can't," she repeated pulling from him and climbing out of the bed.

"Why not?" he asked furiously, standing next to her now.

"I can't commit to anyone. People will get hurt if I don't complete this job."

"What do you mean?"

"Bash, just leave things the way they are, please," she begged him as she turned around and went into the bathroom.

He was angry with her. Twice he had offered his blood to her and twice she had denied him. No one had ever denied anything to him. He quickly dressed and walked out of the room and back to his room.

He paced the floor of his room trying to understand what could possibly be holding her back. Then he remembered her statement and wondered what she could have meant by it. He walked into the bathroom for a quick shower, dried himself off and walked back into the bedroom naked. He got dressed, grabbed his phone from the nightstand and walked out of the room.

CHAPTER EIGHT

ELENA COULDN'T BELIEVE THE emptiness she felt. For the last two nights, Bash hadn't shown up in the gym. She couldn't understand how he was already so deep in her heart. She felt miserable and lonely.

She looked at her phone call list and crossed off the last company name she had just called. She would make one last call and return a couple of voicemail messages. There was a knock on her door. She climbed out of bed and opened the door. She found herself looking at Bash. She was happy to see him.

"Hi," he said.

"Hi," she replied.

"A group of us are going to a club in town. I thought you could join us?"

"That's great, thanks."

"Good."

"What time?" she asked.

"Be ready at eleven," he answered.

"Okay."

They stared at each other for a few seconds until she lowered her head. He stepped back from the door, turned around and walked down the hall. She watched him go before she closed the door. She rested her body against the door and banged her head against it. She took a deep breath, let go of the door handle and walked back to the bed.

She pulled her phone out and returned both voicemail messages. Luckily she was able to reach one of the companies. She spoke to them for several minutes, going over what she needed from them. After a few minutes she ended the call, happy with the results.

She moved to the closet and pulled out the new dress she had bought, hoping to have a chance to go dancing. She loved music and dancing. She and James used to go at least twice a month. They made a great team.

She pulled the dress out, got a pair of shoes that matched and picked out some jewelry to complete the outfit including the pendant necklace her father gave her. She was very pleased with the effect as she twirled in front of the mirror.

She double-checked the to-do list, shut down the laptop and put it back in her carry case. She went into the bathroom for a fast shower, dried off and wrapped the robe around herself. She fixed her hair in a loose bun, pulling several strands down both sides of her face and then applied her makeup. She walked to the bed and sat down on the edge. She made sure there was still plenty of time left to get ready before she pulled her two extra phones from the drawer to check them for messages.

She listened to her leader's voicemail—his message was typically nasty and full of threats. On her other phone she saw that her sister had sent a text message. She read it and replied. She waited for a moment, making sure it went through, then shut off both phones and put them back in the drawer. She pulled a clutch from the drawer and put her phone, money, ID and lip gloss in it. She pulled a satiny shawl from another drawer and dropped it on the bed.

After making sure she had everything she needed, she got dressed. She put her shoes on, wrapped the shawl around her shoulders, picked up her clutch and walked out of the room.

Sebastian was waiting for her in the foyer with Julian and another couple. When he saw her coming down, his breath caught in his lungs. She looked stunningly gorgeous. Her dress just barely covered her butt, showing off her long, finely defined legs. Then he saw the beautiful necklace accentuating her cleavage. Intriguingly enough it was the same design as the tattoo. He pushed this thought to the back of his mind, intending to ask her about it later. She walked over to him and stopped. "Hi," she said to everyone.

"Hi, that's a beautiful necklace," Sebastian said as he looked into her eyes and saw the longing in them.

"Thank you."

He smiled at her, took her hand, entwining his fingers with hers, and together they walked out of the mansion. They reached the car parked in front and he opened the front passenger door for her. She got in while the others climbed in the back. Sebastian got in the driver's side and quickly drove off. Within fifteen minutes they arrived in town. He parked the car across from the club and went around opened the door for her as the others got out. He grabbed her hand and the group crossed the street. He let go of her hand and wrapped an arm around her waist, pulling her tightly to him. She lifted her eyes to him and gave him a big smile. He pressed a soft kiss to her temple as they continued to walk. The group made it to the front of the club where the front door attendant let them in without hesitation. They only had to walk down a short hallway before they were in the club's main hall. The club was fairly large, the lighting soft around the corners and shady on the dance floor. The dance floor was in the center surrounded by tables and chairs. The bar was situated against a large wall.

The club was lively that night and Elena found the music exciting. The five of them walked to the far end and found a large table. Elena sat on a chair facing the dance floor and Sebastian sat next to her, while the others sat across from them. Right away a waitress came over for their order. Elena waited for everyone else to order first and then she ordered a beer for herself.

She very much enjoyed the music, tapping her feet on the floor along with the beat. The other couple got up from their chairs and moved to the dance floor. She watched as they moved to the music. The waitress came back with the drinks and Sebastian placed her beer in front of her. She picked it up and took a sip.

After some time, Julian got up and walked over to a table full of men. Elena could see that he knew them because they laughed with him. She and Sebastian sat drinking, just watching people dance.

Elena was getting anxious; she wanted to be on the floor dancing. After several minutes, Julian came back to the table. "Hey, how about a dance?" he asked, reaching for her hand.

Elena smiled and got up from her chair. She pulled the shawl from her shoulders and dropped it on the back of her chair. "Wow, you look fantastic," he said letting her walk by him.

He moved next to her and placed his hand on her lower back, which was pretty much bare. Sebastian's eyes never left her, but he could sense the eyes of every man and vampire in the room on her. Elena's body moved with the music. Julian watched as her hips swayed. His eyes glided over her body. She looked up at him and smiled.

When the song was over, Julian walked her back to the table. He sat down and took a large sip of his beer. Elena grabbed her beer and took a sip too. Julian finished his beer and went over to the bar; Sebastian joined him.

While the two brothers were talking at the bar, a very attractive vampire approached the table and asked Elena to dance. Elena got up and moved to the dance floor with him. As they started to dance, he moved closer to her and said something in her ear. Elena laughed at what he said. After a few seconds a friend of his joined them, dancing behind her.

Elena wasn't used to attracting men or vampires. She could feel his hands on her back. She continued dancing, but his touch did nothing for her. She swayed her hips side to side as the vampire behind her moved closer and the one in front put his hands on her hips and also moved closer.

She was surprised when she twirled around and saw Bash standing behind the guy in back of her, tapping him on the shoulder. He tilted his head at him and pointed for him to go. The vampire seemed to recognized him and scurried off the floor. In front of her, Elena could see her dance partner's eyes widen in alarm. Bash moved closer to her, grabbed her hips and moved with the music. Elena saw the young vampire hurriedly walk by them.

"Bash," she said punching him on his shoulder, "you scared them away."

"Good," he said smiling at her.

"No one will ask me to dance now."

"Great, you're done with them for the rest of the night," he said pulling her tightly against his body.

Together they swayed their hips creating fantastic friction that engulfed their bodies in the sweetest sensation. They danced for several songs, never letting go of each other. Elena's body was tingling everywhere; they could sense each other's arousal.

Bash stopped dancing, grabbed her hand and walked off the dance floor. He led her to the back of the club and found a bench in a dark corner. He sat down, bringing her onto his lap. Elena turned and straddled his lap as he took her lips between his. He continued kissing and pushing her hips, stroking his erection. She shifted her hips back and forth, feeling a delicious pressure between her legs.

Bash stopped kissing her and pushed the skimpy material aside that covered her breasts and brought his mouth to one of her nipples.

Elena groaned out loud as she rested her head on his shoulder. He continued teasing her breasts, switching between them. He gave a gentle tug on one, lifting his hips to match her motion. He worked her body until she shook uncontrollably in his arms. "Babe, unzip my pants," he said.

"Bash, we shouldn't do this here," she said.

"Elena, now," he insisted.

Elena moved her hands down to his pants and did as he asked. She pushed her hand inside his pants, "You went commando," she observed, stroking him from the tip down to the base.

Bash growled and pushed his hips into her touch. "Pull it out, sweetie."

She let go of his cock, opened his pants wider and pulled his cock out. She went back to stroking him. Sebastian pushed his hand under her dress and ripped her thong off. "Bash," she squealed.

"Put it inside you."

Elena lifted her butt from his lap and she scooped closer to him. She positioned his cock tip at her pussy entrance and slowly drove down on him. He grasped her hips letting her move at her own pace. He clenched his teeth and banged his head back into the bench with a look of pure torture on his face. Finally she got him completely inside her. She pulled up then fast down again.

He held her hips as she found her rhythm, pulling up and swaying her pelvis forward bringing him deeper inside her. He went back to one of her breasts taking it deep in his mouth. She moaned out loud as she dropped her head back. He moved his mouth to the other nipple.

"Bash," she murmured as another moan came out.

"I got you, babe," he said going back to her breast while holding her hips and thrusting hard and fast inside her. He pumped her fast for several minutes then pushed harder and deeper as he grazed her nipple with his teeth. Elena reached her orgasm, moaning and groaning out loud as he continued plunging inside her. Seconds later, he screamed as he blasted his cum inside her. They moved in one motion rubbing and swaying against each other. Elena's body continued to tremble in his arms as she dropped her head on his shoulder, breathing hard. "I can't get enough of you. That was amazing."

"Yes," she agreed between breaths.

Bash pulled a handkerchief from his blazer pocket, lifted her from his lap and cleaned their juices from her thighs, then cleaned himself, putting his soft cock back in his pants. Elena wiggled her dress down her hips and sat straight up on the bench. She nestled close to him and captured his lips, which he quickly opened for her. She launched her tongue in his mouth and spurred a wild duel of tongues.

Suddenly she sensed someone standing in front of them. They both stopped kissing and looked up at the person. "If you two are done the group is ready to go," said Julian.

Elena hid her face in his chest, "You don't think they know what we did," she whispered into his chest.

"Oh, yes, we know," said Julian. "Everyone knows."

"Oh my God," she said mortified.

"Stop teasing her," yelled Bash.

"Sorry, it's too easy."

Elena looked around the bench for her clutch and shawl.

"Looking for these?" asked Julian.

She had forgotten that she left them behind at the other table. "Yes," she said.

Bash stood from the bench bringing her up too. He took the shawl from Julian and helped her put it on. Julian handed her the clutch. Bash wrapped an arm around her waist and brought her body tight against his. Julian went to his other side and walked beside him. They walked through the club to the front hall where they met the others and together they all walked out of the club.

Chapter Nine

Sebastian had never felt so happy—his life was complete with Elena in it. The fact that in another month he was due to mate with Klara was still very much in his mind, but even that couldn't dampen the happiness in his heart. Elena still refused to drink his blood, but he knew that it was only a matter of time before he could change her mind. He shook his head and brought his focus back to the meeting.

He was in Alexandria and had just finished a business meeting with the team leaders. They were all completely in agreement with him regarding vampire matters. When they concluded the meeting, everyone moved to the hall for a bit of entertainment and dancing. Sebastian moved around the hall socializing and chatting with everyone. He stopped for a moment wondering what Elena was doing. Julian reached him and together they mingled with their people.

Back at the mansion, Elena couldn't believe that she had been in Leesville for a month. She was definitely glad she had made the decision to come early to get the preparations for the ceremony underway. Things were going quite well. She was very happy that the ceremony plans were completed ahead of schedule and that the king and Klara were so pleased with her work. She was confident that her plan to alert the vampire council of the attempt to kill the king was progressing smoothly. The vampire network's IT wiz hadn't been able to locate her or stop her from continually blowing through their firewalls. She also felt optimistic that soon she would get her family to safety. Elena finished dressing, then settled in bed and opened her laptop to check for new emails.

Elena worked on her laptop for several hours until she could feel dawn coming through her window. She closed her laptop and put it on her nightstand. She shut off the light and lay back on the bed. She was restless; she missed Bash and on top of that she was starting to crave his blood. Every time he drank from her, her body wanted to taste his blood too, but she couldn't take that step.

She was having nightmares again. She tossed around in her sleep, then something startled her awake. She sat up and listened for what had woken her up. Now she could hear the persistent ring of her phone. She opened the drawer and pulled it out. She looked at the phone and saw that it was her little sister calling her. "Hello," she said.

"Elena," she could hear the despair in her sister's voice.

"Ayla, what's wrong?" she asked.

"It's Mom," her sister said.

"What?"

Her sister didn't answer right away.

"Ayla, tell me," yelled Elena.

"She's been edgy and cranky for days. I think she is going through withdrawals."

"Damn," she said, "You think she needs human blood?"

"Yes, I don't know what to do. She could go back to her old ways."

Elena's mind went back to the ugly memories when her mother would go out into the street, selling her body for human blood.

"Elena, you still there?"

"Yes, I'll take care of it. Give me a couple of hours."

"What are you going to do?"

"I'll get a human donor for her."

"How?" her sister asked her.

"Never mind. Just keep her at home. I'll send someone over. Just keep her home, okay?"

"Okay."

Elena jumped out of bed, quickly got dressed and grabbed her backpack from the closet. She put her tablet, wallet and the three phones in it and grabbed her leather jacket from the chair. Outside the mansion, the sun was still high in the sky but she couldn't waste any time. She pulled her sunglasses from her jacket and put them on. She reached the garage, climbed on a motorcycle and drove off.

She drove down the driveway then caught Highway 171 towards Alexandria. She needed to get there soon so she drove faster than usual. She reached Alexandria in an hour and a half. She looked for the library, hoping that it was still open.

She parked the bike, walked into the library and found a vacant computer. She sat down and working her magic, she accessed her bank account and transferred funds from different accounts. She worked around several routes, making sure that back in Russia no one could see what she was doing. She shifted from account to account several times covering her tracks. It would take hours, maybe even days for anyone to discover her activities, if they ever did.

When she was finished, she closed all the accounts and logged out of the system. She shut the computer off, then pulled out the phone she used to contact her sister and dialed the phone number of her best friend James. The phone rang twice before he picked up. "Elena?" he said.

"Hi James," she said. "Listen, I have to make this quick."

"Okay."

"I transferred money to the account. I need you to get a human donor to my mother, pronto. Can you do it?"

"Yes, no problem."

"Great, also let's move up the completion of the papers. I want to make sure your brother and my family are all ready to go in two weeks." She heard silence on the other end of the phone, "James?"

"Sorry, that soon?"

"We have to. We can't take the chance that Arnav will discover our plan."

"Fine, I'll get everything going."

"Great, keep me updated with your progress. I'll let you go so you can get to Mom."

"I will. Yes, I'll do that right away.

"James, thanks. Talk to you soon."

Elena hung up the phone then sent her sister a quick message. She waited to make sure it went through, then she clicked the phone off and put it in her backpack. She put her leather jacket back on and grabbed her backpack, walking out of the library. While she was inside the library, dusk had approached. She pulled the keys out and started the bike.

She sat on the bike for a while wondering what she could do to alleviate her craving for human blood. She decided to drive around the area and see if she could find a club or bar. She drove around downtown for another hour. Feeling hopeless, she was just about to give up when something or someone made her turn around, and on the next block, she found a little dive bar.

She parked the bike across from the bar and crossed the street. She sat on an empty stool at the bar. The bartender came over and cleaned the countertop in front of her. "Hey," he said.

"Hi," she replied.

"What can I get for you?" he asked.

"Beer, please."

"Be right back."

She twirled on the stool, slowly eyeing her surroundings. She turned back around when the bartender came back with her beer. He slid the beer towards her and she grabbed it quickly. She took a sip from the beer and put it down.

She drank it slowly, looking for a vampire who could help her get what she needed. She finished the first beer and ordered another. The bartender came back with it and she took a large gulp and placed it back on the bar. She sat at the bar for some time with no luck. A tremor ran through her body—she was getting desperate for blood.

She was on her fourth beer, and so far, no one of interest had showed up. She finished the beer, and as she pulled some money out of her pocket to pay the bill she sensed the presence of another vampire. Elena turned her body towards the entryway. Standing there looking around the bar was a nice-looking young man.

Their eyes met and he gave her a smile as he walked towards her. She stared at him as he walked over and sat down on the empty stool next to her. She signaled the bartender for two more beers.

"Hi, I'm Nick," the young vampire said, picking up the beer and taking a sip.

"Hi, my name's Elena." she said. They both stayed quiet for a moment drinking the beers.

"I hope you can help me," she stated looking at him.

"Maybe," he said smiling.

She took another sip of her beer before speaking again. She leaned closer to him and whispered, "I'm looking for a human donor."

"Okay."

"Can you help?"

"Yes. It will cost you though," he said.

"I've got the money. No drugs or alcohol in the system."

He looked into her eyes for a second then said, "Give me an hour."

"You've got fifteen minutes or no deal."

He waited for some time before replying to her, "I don't know."

"Fifteen minutes and I'll pay you double for your services."

He thought it over, "Fine, fifteen minutes. Let me make some calls."

He moved off of the stool and walked to the back of the bar to make his calls. She watched him as he walked away, then turned to the bar and continued to drink her beer. Minutes later he came back and sat next to her.

"All set," he said grabbing his beer and taking a sip.

They sat together making small talk. She bought him another beer while she nervously twirled her beer bottle. When the fifteen minutes were up, she stood up from the stool and pulled some money out of her pocket.

"Wait," he said grasping her arm, "He's here," he said turning his face to the entryway.

She followed his gaze and saw a tall handsome young man walking towards them. She went to sit back on the stool when he stopped her.

"No, let's go to a table," he said motioning toward the other side of the room.

She paid the bill and walked with him as Nick caught up with them. The donor found a secluded table in the dark corner. They all sat down. "Let's make this simple. You know what I want."

"Yes. I'm Sam," he said.

"Elena. How much?

"One hundred," said Sam.

"Okay. Where?" she asked.

"I'm friends with the owner; you can use the back room," said Nick.

"Good, let's go. You'll get paid when I'm done."

They all stood up and Nick walked towards the back, followed by Elena and Sam. She kept herself alert to her surroundings. Nick opened the door, turned the light on and walked in with the other two still behind him. Elena checked out the room. There was a bed in the corner with a nightstand across from a small sofa, and opposite that was a small table with two chairs.

She turned to face them. "No tricks or I'll cut off his head," she said.

"Deal," Sam said.

Nick walked out of the room closing the door behind him. Sam moved towards the bed. "No, the sofa," she said.

Elena dropped her backpack on the floor then pulled her jacket off and laid it down on the sofa. Sam moved next to her as he checked out her body, slowly gazing up and down her form.

"Sit," she said dryly.

Elena didn't trust anyone, so she reached for a chair and jammed it under the doorknob. While she did that, Sam pulled his shirt off and sat down. Elena looked at him; he was good-looking but his body did nothing for her. She sat next to him, and he reached for her, caressing her arm with his finger. "No, just blood."

"I can give you so much more," he said still stroking her arm.

"No," she snapped pulling her arm away.

He settled back on the sofa and rested his head back, moving it sideways to give her access to his throat. Elena got closer to him and placed a hand on his chest. She extended her fangs and dipped her head toward his neck. She bit down and drank from him, closing her eyes as she savored his blood.

Sam moaned under her touch. He unzipped his pants, pulled his cock out and stroked himself. He rubbed his body against her arm. She kept drinking from him for several minutes until she could feel the craving diminish. As she drank, Sam pumped faster until his body was just about to climax. Elena drank for another two minutes as Sam exploded. Elena retracted her fangs and licked the pinpricks to close them. Sam pulled a bandana from his pants pocket and cleaned himself.

Elena's body was flushed but she was feeling better. Now all she was thinking about was having Sebastian inside her. She stood up from the sofa and pulled the money from her pocket to pay Sam.

Sam was buttoning his shirt. He stopped at the last button and took the money, put it in his back pocket, then finished buttoning his shirt. He put his cock inside his pants and zipped up. Elena put her jacket on, pulled the chair from the door and opened it. She stood in the doorway waiting for Sam.

They walked together down the hall and back to the table where Nick was sitting alone. She pulled the money out of her jacket and handed it to him.

"Thank you," he said putting the money in his shirt pocket.

Sam sat down beside Nick, leaving her standing by herself. Elena waved her hand at them, stopping for a moment at the bar. She pulled a hundred dollar bill out and slipped it into the bartender's shirt pocket. "Thanks," she said as she walked out of the bar.

Sebastian walked through the door happy that he was back home. The meeting went well but they still couldn't pinpoint who was behind the alleged assassination attempt. He and Julian were angry that the investigation was going nowhere. He quickly went up the stairs and directly to Elena's room. He opened the door and found the room empty, her bedclothes were on the floor and her bed was unmade. He walked out of the room and closed the door. Back downstairs, he asked the group if they had seen her. Everyone said no. He walked out of the room and down the hall to the gym. He opened the door and saw a couple of men training. He left the gym and walked towards the entertainment room.

Sebastian left the entertainment room with a serious expression on his face. Again, no one had seen Elena. He walked to Julian's office where he knew his brother was doing paperwork. He didn't knock, but just opened the door. Julian looked up from the paperwork in front of him. "Really, haven't you spent enough time with me yet?" he asked sarcastically. Sebastian didn't find his little brother amusing.

CHAPTER TEN

JULIAN COULD SEE THAT Sebastian was upset about something. He was pacing in front of his desk saying nothing. "Bash, man, stop pacing and tell me what's wrong."

Sebastian stopped and stared at him, "I can't find Elena," he yelled.

"What? Did you check her room?" he asked.

"Yes, also the living room, gym and entertainment room."

"Maybe she's outside in the garden."

"Maybe. Call the security desk and ask the guard to check the cameras."

"Okay."

Julian picked up the phone and made the call. He talked to them for several minutes. Sebastian listened with a grim expression on his face. Julian hung up the phone.

"She's not in the garden. They'll check earlier times to see if they can tell where she went. They'll call me back. Sit. You're making me crazy."

Sebastian gave his brother a hard look then stopped pacing and sat down. After they sat in silence for several minutes there was a knock on the door. "Come in," said Julian.

The head of security walked in the room. He approached them. "My lord, Julian," he said.

"Tom," said Julian.

"Any news?" asked Sebastian.

"I had my team check the footage from the past three hours but they found nothing. Then I called all my staff. The security guard at the gate had a written report from the human guard that Elena left in a hurry this afternoon."

"You mean early tonight," corrected Sebastian.

"No, my lord, I mean early today. According to the time in the report she left around 3:00 pm. No one thought anything of it, but the guard thought she was acting nervous so he made the report. Here let me show you."

He moved behind the desk and opened the surveillance program on his tablet. Sebastian moved in back of Julian's chair. Tom found the specific time in the report and ran the video. "There," he said pointing her out on the screen.

Julian couldn't believe his eyes: There she was in the middle of the afternoon out in the sun. He did notice that she seemed nervous. They watched until she was out of site, then Tom stopped the video. "My lord, there is no report of her coming back yet."

"Thanks Tom," said Julian.

"Let me know the instant she shows up. Hold her at the gate," Sebastian ordered.

"We will, sire."

Tom walked out of the office and Sebastian went back to pacing. "Where the fuck could she be?" he yelled.

"Sebastian sit," snapped Julian.

"No."

Sebastian stopped pacing and crossed his arms across his chest and stared at Julian. Julian just stared back.

Elena quickly crossed the street, got on the bike and drove off. She cruised along for a couple of blocks then found the exit for Highway 171. She took the exit, set a safe speed and headed back to the mansion.

After about forty-five minutes, she grew tired of driving. She shifted a bit on the bike trying to get her back muscles loose. She drove for another half an hour then she saw the highway sign with the exit she needed. She had two more miles to go on the highway and probably another five before she got back to the mansion. She picked up speed, took her exit and quickly found herself driving on the road towards the house.

She turned into the driveway and took a deep breath of relief to be back. When she drove up to the gate, the guard came out of the gatehouse towards her. Elena stopped beside him. "Elena, I need you to park the bike over there," he said pointing to an empty space inside the gate, "Wait for me there."

Elena didn't like him ordering her around but she didn't say anything. He went back to the gatehouse and opened the gate. Elena drove her bike forward and, as soon as she had enough space to maneuver the bike, she took off. She didn't look behind her but picked up speed and drove up the driveway. She could hear the guard calling after her. She got to the garage, shut off the bike, jumped off and ran out of the garage and around the back of the house.

Sebastian couldn't sit there any longer. He was walking out of the office when he heard a knock on the door. He reached the door and opened it. "Tom."

"My lord, she's here but we have a problem."

"What problem?" Julian asked. Sebastian was now standing next to him.

"She ignored the order from the guard at the gate and drove off. He saw her going towards the garage, but she was going too fast for him to follow her. He called it in right away."

"Goddamn it," yelled Sebastian.

"I've already called for guards to check the garage."

"Let's go," said Sebastian, hastening out of the office. He hurried down the hall towards the foyer. As they reached the foyer one of the guards walked up to them. "My lord, she's not in the garage."

"Damn it."

"We have every available guard looking for her," said Tom.

"I'll help with the search," said Sebastian.

"Me too," said Julian.

As they started to move, Sebastian heard a commotion behind them.

"Let go of me, you asshole," yelled Elena to the guard who was forcefully pulling her by the arm toward the foyer.

"Let her go," screamed Sebastian, rushing to her.

Immediately the guard let go of her arm as Sebastian reached her. He stopped in front of her and his face turned hard. He sniffed her and instantly let out a menacing growl. Julian moved next to her.

"Sebastian stop," he said with a firm voice.

"Elena, what the fuck is going on?" Sebastian screamed.

"Why don't you tell me? I'm the one being manhandled," she yelled back pushing away from the guards.

Just as he was about to speak, Tom walked into the foyer and interrupted him.

"My king, I've received a call from the gate guard. We have two European vampires requesting sanctuary," said Tom.

"What?" Sebastian and Julian said together as they turned to him.

Elena couldn't believe what she had just heard. Tom had just called Bash "My king." He was looking straight at Bash, not at the man she had believed was the king. Bash was the fucking king! This whole time she had been played for a fool. She started to fidget, but her face was hard and devoid of all emotion. She turned slightly and took two steps away from Bash, making a break for the stairs. "Elena, don't move," Sebastian yelled.

Elena stopped and turned around to face him. She locked eyes with him, her stare drilling through him. Her eyes were quickly turning red.

"Elena, go to Julian's office and wait for me there," he ordered her, furiously.

"Julian? Who's Julian?" she responded never taking her eyes from him.

Everyone around him was completely stunned and stared at Elena in disbelief. Sebastian quickly stood in front of her. Elena didn't back away from Sebastian, but she had to lift her face now as she kept staring hard into his eyes.

"He's my brother, Elena," he informed her through clenched teeth, leaning toward her face.

"Tom, have the guards bring the two men to my office, and have the guards stay with them. I'll be there in a minute," Sebastian ordered, turning briefly from her.

He took her by her arm and pulled her down the hall. He didn't speak to her while they were walking. He opened Julian's office door and pushed her in, "Don't move. Wait for me," he brusquely ordered her. Elena turned furiously from him and stomped in the office as he slammed the door close.

Sebastian stood at the door holding onto the knob. The stench of the human on her had brought him to verge of snapping. He took deep breaths then walked back to the foyer where Julian was waiting for him. Everyone else had left. The two brothers walked down the hall to Sebastian's office. Sebastian walked behind his desk and sat down as Julian came around the desk and stood next to him. The two vampires looked at them. They stood in silence guarded by the two men.

"So you two are requesting sanctuary. On what grounds?" Sebastian asked.

"My king, on the grounds of our leader's misconduct," answered one of them.

"Let's hear your story," said Julian.

Sebastian and Julian quietly listened to the vampires' story. After they finished talking, Julian moved to stand behind them. Sebastian stared hard at them, thinking the situation through. Maybe they could use this to their advantage.

"Okay, you can stay with us. We'll need to investigate your allegations, but you're welcome in my home. Julian, find them rooms."

"Okay, I'll make the call."

"Thank you," they both said.

"The guards will stay with you until someone comes to get you," said Sebastian moving from behind the desk and walking out of the room.

Elena was in Julian's office pacing like a caged animal. She had the start of a major headache from trying to figure this out. She couldn't believe that Sebastian was the king and that he had lied to her. *How could she be so stupid? Why had she assumed that Julian was the king?*

She stopped pacing and dragged a hand down her face in frustration. This was an added complication that she wasn't expecting. "What the fuck," she said slamming her hand on the back of a chair.

74

Elena couldn't stand this tension any longer; she had to get away. She moved to the door and furiously opened it. She rushed out and slammed into a hard body.

Sebastian reached his hands out for her but she reacted quickly and stepped away from him. There was nowhere else to go, so she went back into the office. "What the fuck?" she yelled.

"What the fuck. Really? Where were you?" Sebastian asked furiously stomping behind her.

"It's none of your business," she snapped back.

"You're my business. Everything about you is my business."

"No, let me go," she said moving forward trying to get away from him.

Sebastian stepped in front of her cutting off her exit.

"You lied to me," she said turning away from him, moving closer to the desk.

"Where did you go? Who were you with?" he asked rushing her.

"Sebastian," Julian called.

"Oh my God. How could I have been so stupid? You told me your name was Bash," she whispered as she tried to move away. But she didn't have anywhere to go because he took up every inch of space.

Sebastian quickly grabbed her arms. "You're my woman. You deny my offer to drink my blood, then you dare go to someone else," he screamed shaking her.

"I can't take your blood," she said.

"Why not?"

Elena didn't answer him right away. She couldn't face him. Julian stood back and watched them argue.

"Elena," Sebastian warned.

"Where did you go?"

"Damn it, I went to Alexandria. I needed to do some personal banking," she said.

"Why not tell me?"

"It was a last-minute decision."

"Was it a last-minute decision to drink from someone, too?"

"Yes, I needed to get rid of this craving," she stated, trying to step away with no luck.

"What craving?" he asked.

"Never mind," she snapped.

Sebastian forced her to turn her face and looked at him. "What craving?"

"Bash, please," she begged him.

"Elena," he screamed slamming his hand on the desk. "What craving?"

Elena jumped but couldn't get away from him. He had a tight grip on her arm. "Your blood, okay?"

"You crave my blood but instead you decide to go to someone else?" he asked furiously.

"Sebastian," Julian said warning him, moving closer to them.

"Yes," was all she said to him.

"Did you sleep with him?"

"No," she answered instantly.

Elena didn't know what to do, she stood there just staring at his back.

"Go to your room. Go wash his stench from your body," he ordered her.

"You can't tell me what to do," she barked back.

"Yes I can, as your man and your king."

Elena started to say something but then closed her mouth. She lowered her head down but not before yelling back him, "My king, fuck you."

"Elena!" yelled Julian now standing behind her.

Elena kept her head down as she turned around and stepped by Julian.

"Elena, I'll be there later. Now go," Sebastian commanded, waving his hand at her.

She walked away, opened the door and walked out, stomping her feet all the way to her room. When she got there she walked in and slammed the door. "Who the fuck does he think he is?" she said out loud, pacing her room. "He's the king, that's who he is," she answered herself, banging her hand on the side of the bureau.

76

She pulled her bag off and banged it hard on the chair, then did the same with her jacket. She sat down on the edge of the bed, pulled her boots off and furiously threw them against the wall.

As Elena was working herself into a temper, Sebastian was still in Julian's office. He was trying to make sense of everything Elena had told him.

"What do you think you're doing with her? In less than a month, you're getting mated. Do you plan to keep her?" stated Julian.

"Yes. No. Maybe. What the fuck?" Sebastian yelled in his face.

"You can't do this to Klara. She's a good woman. She doesn't deserve this," snapped Julian, holding his ground and staring at his brother.

Sebastian stared back at him, "If you're so fond of her, why don't you mate with her?" he snapped, stepping away and rubbing his face with his hand in desperation.

"What? That's crazy," argued Julian, throwing his arms up the air.

"Wait. That's it! You will mate with her," he said with new hope in his voice.

"No, you can't. She's expecting to mate a king."

"Yes, I can. I'm the king. I can do anything I want. Besides, she's expecting to mate into the family. You're my brother and second in command."

"You can't decide this without talking to her first."

"Fine, we'll talk to her tomorrow night."

"Sebastian."

"Julian."

"Fine, we'll talk to her tomorrow."

Sebastian moved to the door, opened it and quickly walked out.

In her room, Elena was still pacing the floor. She went to unbutton her pants, but then stopped. "I don't have to do anything," she said out loud.

She stood in the middle of the room for a few seconds just thinking. She began to pace again when all of a sudden the door opened. She stopped in her tracks as Sebastian walked into the room.

Sebastian looked her over and noticed that she was still dressed. His temper flared again as he rushed to her. "I told you to shower," he roared in front of her now.

"No," she snapped back, lifting her face to look at him.

"Elena, get in the shower before I tear the clothes from you and put you in it myself."

Elena took a step back, "Don't you dare touch me."

"Elena," he warned her, losing his patience.

"No," she snapped again crossing her arms below her breasts propping them up with the unconscious effect of showing more of her cleavage.

Sebastian kicked his shoes off and pulled his socks off. He dragged his t-shirt over his shoulder, dropping it on the floor, then quickly pushed his pants and brief down his legs and kicked them off. He stood naked in front of her. He moved toward her.

Elena propelled her arms out in front of her, "Don't," was all she was able to say as he pushed her arms away as he grabbed her blouse and ripped it off her.

Elena was completely stunned by his actions but her body reacted differently. She could feel the ache between her legs now.

"Bash, or whatever your name is, stop," she yelled trying to get his attention.

Sebastian brusquely ripped her pants off her. Elena stood in front of him in just her bra and thong. He lifted her over his shoulder and walked to the bathroom. "Let me go," she said kicking her legs and punching his back.

He moved to the stall and turned on the water. He stood her on the floor and, with one swift move, ripped off her bra and thong. He grabbed her hand and pulled her with him into the shower. Elena didn't know what to do.

"I can't stand the stench of this man on you," he said picking up a cloth from the shelf, putting some shower gel on it and roughly washing her.

Elena stopped struggling against him and let him wash her. By the time he was finished she was breathing hard; his hands on her made her crazy. He poured shampoo into his hand and moved closer to her to wash her hair. Elena leaned her head on his chest and closed her eyes.

When he was done washing her hair, he brought her back under the water and rinsed her hair and body. Elena wrapped her arms around his waist and pulled herself against him. He had a huge hard on just from washing her; she could feel it pressing on her stomach.

Sebastian turned the shower off, turned her around and pressed her back to the wall. He grabbed her butt and lifted her up. "Insert my cock in your pussy, babe," he said in her ear.

Elena moved one hand between their bodies, took hold of his cock and did as he said. He thrust hard and deep inside her. Elena wrapped her arms around his neck and her legs around his waist and held tight. He pumped hard, slamming deep inside her every time. He pushed her hair from her neck, bit down on her neck and drank from her.

Her orgasm slammed hard, her body convulsing desperately on his arms. He continued pumping her pussy and, in seconds, he erupted inside her. He kept moving until her trembling ceased.

With his cock still semi-hard inside her, he walked out of the shower stall, out of the bathroom and back into the room. Elena held tightly onto his neck. He moved to the bed and without letting go of her butt, he settled her on the bed. Elena could feel his cock inside her starting to get hard again. He laid her down and moved slowly in and out of her. He lowered his head to one of her breasts and pulled her nipple into his mouth, twirling his tongue, tugging and nipping softly. Elena's body was dissolving under him; she melted into his touch.

"Sebastian," she murmured between moans, her eyes closed.

"Elena, open your eyes. Look at me," he said biting on her nipple.

Elena opened her eyes and looked into his. She wrapped her legs around his waist.

"You're mine. Don't you ever forget it," he said biting her other nipple and thrusting hard inside her. He moved his mouth towards her neck as Elena gazed into his eyes. She tilted her face to the side, opening her neck for him. Instantly he dipped down and bit into her. He drank from her as he moved faster in and out. In seconds her body erupted into another explosive orgasm.

Elena's whole body shuddered under him. She held onto his arms, digging her nails into them. His thrusts became shorter and deeper and, in seconds, he came for the second time inside her. He slowed down as he stopped drinking from her and licked the puncture wounds closed. He stopped thrusting but didn't pull out from inside her. Elena let her legs drop from his waist. He moved his body to the side, taking the weight from her body. He wrapped an arm around her waist holding her body to his. After a few seconds she could feel his cock inside her getting hard again. She closed her eyes. The sensation of him getting big and hard inside her was incredibly erotic. She pushed her hips up taking him deeper.

Sebastian moved his arm from her waist under her butt and flipped her over. Now she was on top of him, straddling his hips. Elena stayed still for a moment.

"Look at me. Move, babe," he said already completely hard and tight inside her.

Elena lifted herself up then pushed back down. She looked into his eyes and saw the shine in them. She found a nice rhythm and kept moving up and down, swaying her pelvis back and forth.

He was on the verge of coming, and she was experiencing pure torture. He moved his hands to her hips and stopped her from moving. "Sebastian," she protested.

He slowly thrust up holding her still. "Drink from me," he demanded.

Elena shook her head sideways. He moved one of his hands to the back of her neck forcing her down. He brought her face to his chest. "Drink," he demanded again, keeping her face against him.

Elena's body was engulfed with desire; she held herself still, savoring the sensation of his cock moving inside her while he softly stroked her back. Still he did not let her go. "Drink, now," he yelled.

Elena couldn't stop her fangs from elongating. She hesitated for only a second before she bit down on his chest and drank his blood. Sebastian's body instantly reacted to her; he was ready to come. He pumped faster, moving his hand from her neck and found her clit. He rubbed hard and, in seconds, they exploded in unison.

She drank from him for several minutes after. Her trembles diminished, leaving her body with a delicious humming sensation all over. She stopped drinking from him and closed the bite wounds with her tongue. She laid her head down on his chest and closed her eyes, enjoying the aftermath of their lovemaking.

Sebastian pulled out from inside her, and keeping her body beside his, he pulled the covers over them, wrapping an arm under her body and pulling her tighter. Elena kept her eyes closed and her head on his chest.

She could feel the bond building between them already. He gently stroked her lower back. He reached for the lamp and shut off the light. She felt warm and safe in his arms, and soon she felt herself drifting off to sleep.

CHAPTER ELEVEN

SEBASTIAN ABRUPTLY OPENED HIS eyes. He felt tears wet against his chest. He didn't move until his eyes adjusted to the darkness. He moved his hand to touch her, but stopped. Elena was thrashing in his arms.

"Please don't hurt them. I'll do anything you say. I'll do it. Please don't hurt my mother and sister. Please don't. Noooooo," she screamed in a petrified tone as she snapped out of deep sleep into a sitting position.

Elena covered her face with her hands and kept crying. Sebastian embraced her, rocking her back and forth. After a few minutes she stopped crying and all he heard was soft sobbing.

"Elena, you have a mother and sister?" he asked.

Elena moved from his arms and dried her face with the back of her hands. She didn't look at him. "No, I have no family," she answered.

"But..." was all she let him say.

"It was just a nightmare." She turned her back to him and pulled the sheet over her body and closed her eyes.

Sebastian didn't insist, he could feel the pain in her words. He curled behind her, wrapped an arm under her body and pulled her close. Elena didn't fight him. She curled her head on his arm and closed her eyes.

He could feel how tense she was. He placed his other hand on her stomach and gently stroked her. He could feel her body relax, then he heard her slow breathing; she was already back to sleep. Sebastian stopped stroking her stomach but didn't move his hand. He tenderly kissed her head and stayed awake for several minutes to make sure she was okay.

Elena woke up totally wrapped in his body. She tried to move her body away from him, but was only able to move an inch or so.

"What are you doing?" he asked, pulling her back.

"I, I," she didn't know what to say, but she knew she needed to get away from him.

"Elena."

She said the first thing that came into her head, "I have to use the bathroom."

Sebastian pulled his arm back and set her body free. She immediately jumped out of bed and ran to the bathroom. She closed the door and leaned her back against it, taking a deep breath and slowly letting it out. She used the toilet and walked into the shower stall. She put the water on and moved under it.

She stood under the water for a moment with her eyes closed. She could sense him in the bathroom. She kept her eyes closed, but was aware that he had walked into the stall and stood behind her. She leaned back into his body and let a soft sob escape her mouth. Sebastian turned her around and pulled her into his arms. Elena hid her face in his chest. She took a deep breath and stepped away from him. "I'm fine," she said, not looking at him.

She turned around and grabbed the washcloth, pouring some gel on it. He took the cloth from her hand and slowly washed her. After he washed her, he washed himself while she rinsed. Elena moved past him and out of the stall.

Elena grabbed a towel and dried herself. Sebastian did the same beside her. She wrapped the towel around her body and brushed her teeth. Back in her room, she looked at the mess on the floor and picked up her shredded clothes.

"Leave it and I'll have housekeeping take care of it."

"No, I don't want any gossip about me," she said picking up the last piece. She threw them in one of her bags in the closet.

"You want to train?" he asked.

"I can't. I have a fitting for Klara's dress for the ceremony."

"Elena."

"I'm fine," she said pulling an outfit from the closet and laying it on the bed. Sebastian sat on the edge of the bed watching her dress. When she was finished dressing, she combed her hair and worked it into a bun. She put on a little bit of makeup, grabbed the shoulder bag on the chair and pulled her wallet and phone out of it to put in her carry case.

She turned to face him, "I have to go and I don't want to be late," she said.

Sebastian pulled her into his arms and gave her a kiss. He kissed her for some time before he let her go.

Elena sat outside on the terrace, enjoying the night. She knew she had plenty of time before she had to meet Klara. She didn't feel guilty about telling Sebastian she had to leave. She needed time away from him. Elena didn't know how she would react when she saw Klara, knowing that Klara would soon be mating the man she loved.

Sebastian walked into Julian's office to find Klara already there, sitting with Julian on the big sofa. He walked over and sat across from them.

"Hi," said Klara.

"Hi," he said as he looked at Julian.

Klara caught the look between them. "What's wrong?" she asked.

Sebastian hesitated for a moment, then began, "Klara, you know you and I are mating only for the good of the packs."

"Yes."

"I have a proposition for you," he said sitting on the edge of the chair and grabbing her hands between his.

"Okay," she said looking over to Julian.

"I love someone else," he said.

"Elena."

Sebastian and Julian exchanged looks again.

"How do you know?" asked Julian.

"Everyone knows. It's obvious by the way you look at her. Plus after what happened in the club, there was no doubt."

"Fine. Yes, Elena."

"Okay, what's the proposition?"

"Julian will mate you. The packs will still be strong."

Klara turned to face Julian, "Is that okay with you?" she asked.

"Yes, but I want to make sure you're okay with it first."

Klara looked at him silently for a moment. Julian stood up and walked away from her, taking her silence as a rejection. "You don't have to if you don't want to," he said.

Klara stood up and went over to him. She touched his arm. "I want to," she said smiling at him.

"Really?"

"Really," she said.

Sebastian stood up from his chair and patted them both on the back. "Perfect. No one can know about this arrangement."

"But my family…" she started to say.

"Everything will be fine. I'll handle your family. Okay, Klara? Julian? And let's not mention the change in arrangements to Elena just yet."

"Yes," they said together.

"I believe you're late for an appointment with Elena."

Klara looked at her watch, "No, I still have some time left," she said.

Sebastian's face suddenly went hard. "Damn it. She's driving me crazy," he said.

"I'll go. I'll let you two talk," she said starting to walk away.

"Wait. Julian, let's send a guard with them. Use the house car," he said.

"Good idea. I'll call Tom. Okay Klara?"

"Yes," she said walking out of the office.

Sebastian couldn't believe Elena had lied to him again. He sat back down on the chair. Julian came over and sat across from him.

"What now?" Julian asked.

Sebastian looked at him, "She had a nightmare last night. She was crying, pleading with someone not to hurt her family."

"Family? There isn't any record of family in her file. Did you ask her about it?" Julian said.

"I know. Yes, she said she didn't have any family."

"You don't believe her," he observed.

"No, I don't. Please investigate deeper into her background, okay?"

"Okay. I have some work to go over with you. And let's discuss these two new vampires," said Julian.

"Okay."

They moved to the desk. Julian pulled a pile of paperwork from a folder and they smoothly transitioned to business mode and started working.

Elena stayed outside for as long as she could. Just as she was about to get up and go back in the house, two other vampires came out. She looked up at them but didn't say anything. She lowered her head and tried to stay calm. They ignored her and walked down the terrace into the garden.

Elena's heart beat faster; she couldn't believe she knew them. She was so glad she never hung out with the vampires under Arnav. Obviously they didn't recognize her because they just kept walking. "Damn it," she burst out under her breath, wondering what Arnav's game was now.

Elena sat there for another minute, then she got up and walked into the house. She walked through the living room and into the foyer where Klara was already waiting for her.

"Ready?" she said.

"Not yet, I'm waiting for the guard."

"A guard. What for?" she asked.

"Sebastian ordered one to stay with us," she said.

"He did?" she enquired with a frown on her face.

At that moment, one of the guards approached them. "Hi," said the guard, "ready to go?"

"Yes," said Klara.

"Okay," he said letting them walk ahead of him. He opened the door for them and closed it behind him. Elena couldn't believe that they also had someone to drive them. The guard opened the back door of the car for them. Klara got in and Elena followed. The guard got in the front with the driver.

Elena was fuming, but she tried not to show it. She smiled at Klara and sat back in the seat. They rode all the way to the dress shop in silence. The car stopped and the guard opened the door for them. Elena climbed out with Klara behind her. The guard stayed close to them as they walked to the shop. He opened the shop door for them. The store associate brought them to the back where they already had Klara's dress set up for her.

Back at the mansion, Sebastian and Julian were in a meeting with Tom, head of security. He gave them a report of the investigation of the two vampires from Europe. They all agreed that they should be watched carefully. Then Tom pulled out the report on Elena.

"This is the report on your Elena," said Tom.

"My Elena," repeated Sebastian.

"Man, the news is all over about you two. I've never seen you so angry with anyone. Besides, everyone knows about the scene at the club. Every vampire that values his or her life is staying away from her."

"Really, how does everyone know about the club?" he asked, looking at Julian.

"Don't look at me. I didn't say anything," said Julian.

"Anyway," said Tom, "she's the best in her agency, you know that. But did you know that Elena Baich didn't exist before she started working at the agency several years ago? There is no information on her prior to that."

"Nothing?" asked Sebastian.

"Nothing."

"What the hell?" Sebastian snapped.

"Your lady is a mystery," said Tom.

Tom left the file with the reports on Julian's desk and left the office. Sebastian didn't like this news. He was in love with this mystery woman. He needed to talk with her and get her to open up to him.

After an hour at the dress shop, Elena was more than ready to leave. Klara had tried on several other dresses plus the chosen ceremony dress. She gave the associate the instructions for sending the dresses to her. After everything was settled, they walked out of the shop. Elena suggested they go to a small café around the corner. She was definitely not ready to go back to the mansion. They walked to the café and sat down on a corner bench where the guard could see all the doors.

They chatted and laughed for a while, enjoying their coffees. The guard paid the bill and all three walked out of the café. They didn't have to walk back to the shop; the car was already waiting for them outside.

The guard opened the door for them to climb in the back, then closed the door and got in the front. The car drove off. The women sat back in the seats for another silent ride.

Elena wasn't ready to see Sebastian. She walked through the kitchen and out of the house, which brought her to a kitchen garden. She walked for a bit until she found a bench where she sat down and closed her eyes. She was so confused about what the two other vampires from Europe were doing here. But more than that, she was torn between completing her assignment and the strong feelings she had for the man she had been ordered to assassinate.

Sebastian and Julian were in the entertainment room playing pool. Sebastian made his shot and missed. His mind wasn't on the game; he was thinking about Elena again. He moved away for Julian to take his turn. They finished playing the game and, predictably, Julian won.

Sebastian put his pool cue away and walked to the bar where he grabbed another beer. He sat down on a chair with a small group and joined the conversation. He stayed chatting for a while, sipping his beer. When he got up to bring the empty bottle to the bar he saw Klara walk into the room. He brought the bottle to the bar, left it on the countertop and walked over to Klara where she was talking to Julian. "All set with the dress?" he asked.

"Yes," she said with a smile.

"Elena?"

"I don't know. I left her in the foyer."

Sebastian said goodbye to Julian and Klara and left the entertainment room. He walked swiftly up the stairs and to her room. He opened the door but the room was dark. He decided not waste any more time and went down to the security office. He ordered the guard on duty to bring up all the surveillance cameras around the mansion. He took the empty chair next to the guard and watched the screens. They checked all the rooms inside the mansion and then they checked the outside cameras. "There," said Sebastian pointing to the monitor. "Thanks," he said, rushing out of the room.

Sebastian hadn't liked what he saw on the monitor. He ran at vampire speed through the halls and out of the house. He stopped running as he got closer. When he reached her he sat next to her, and taking her hand in his, he brought it to his lips. He softly kissed her palm as she caressed his face with her hand.

"What's wrong?" he asked.

"Nothing," she said."

"Elena, please tell me what's wrong?"

Elena closed her eyes tight, "I can't."

"Why not?" he asked.

"It's complicated."

Sebastian wanted to shake her and demand answers from her and at the same time embrace her. He took a deep breath and ran his hand over his face.

"Uncomplicate it, Elena. Talk to me."

"Sebastian, please," she begged him.

"Fine. Let's go in," he said standing up and pulling her with him.

Elena let him pull her up. He wrapped an arm around her waist and pulled her closer to his body. They walked together through the garden and back into the house. They walked through the living room and up the stairs, but instead of taking her to her room, he walked down the other hall to his room. Elena didn't object.

CHAPTER TWELVE

Suddenly, there were only two weeks left until the mating ceremony. Every time Elena thought of Sebastian getting mated to Klara, her heart ached. He hadn't talked to her about the ceremony or what would happen with them afterward and she didn't bring it up. She knew that the chances of her coming out alive from this situation with Arnav were slim to none.

But once she got her family to safety and out of the leaders' way, she would go after Arnav. She had no choice because she knew he would never stop trying to find a way to hurt her. She also knew that he had developed an obsession with her since the day they met during an event she had planned.

Elena shook her head and cleared it. She would think of what to do next after her family was safe and out of Europe. She needed to stay focused. She had worked hard for the last eleven days, and, as of last night, she was satisfied that everything was in place. She wrote a quick note on her laptop, then closed the program and shut down the computer.

On the other side of the mansion, Sebastian was working on some papers. He entered some information into the computer, then closed the system. Just as he was finishing, Julian walked into his office. "Hey," Julian said, sitting down in one of the chairs across from Sebastian's desk.

"Hi. Any information on Elena?"

"No, nothing. But I've got news on Arnav. He's definitely getting ready for something. The team watching him reported that there has been a lot of activity from his pack."

"Okay. So are we doing something about it?" Sebastian asked.

"What? There's no concrete evidence of any wrongdoing. The team will let us know of any false move as soon as it happens," answered Julian.

"Good. Send a second team to London for back up," he said.

"Okay."

"How are you and Klara doing?"

"Good, I like her a lot and she seems to reciprocate. Have you told Elena?"

"I'm glad. No. Is there any news on the two from Europe?

"No, their story checked out. They seem to get along with everyone. We're still keeping an eye on them."

"Good. Ready with the financial reports?"

"Yes," he said as he started up his tablet to show him the reports.

Back in her room, Elena checked for messages from her sister and best friend James, but there was nothing. She needed to make sure that everything was in place. She would have to find some way to get into town tomorrow. She had been working on last-minute changes to the seating arrangement in her room for most of the night. She needed some fresh air. Deciding to go for a jog, she put on her running clothes and sneakers. She picked up her phone from the nightstand and walked out of her room. She looked for anyone in the hall and took the back stairs, walking at a fast pace until she got out of the house. She walked to the garden farthest from the house and got on the path. As she was jogging, she was glad that the path didn't have too much lighting. She jogged along the path keeping a steady pace.

She thought about Sebastian while jogging. She felt so close to him. They already shared blood three times and every time was the most extraordinary experience. Elena knew she loved him and knowing she would have to leave him was causing her much pain. She never imagined that she would find love; she had been prepared to spend her life alone until Arnav had put her in the predicament she was in now.

She pulled out the phone again and checked for messages—still nothing. She was worried. James was good at keeping her in the loop. She was even more determined to get to town tomorrow. She finished a second round on the path then found a nice grassy area and sat down for a few minutes. She rested her head on her hands, contemplating everything that had happened to her during the past month and a half.

Sebastian finished going through the financial reports with Julian. They agreed to shift some of the investments around. Julian closed the reports and shut his tablet off. He said goodbye to Sebastian and left the office. Sebastian sat quietly in his chair for several minutes thinking about his relationship with Elena. He knew that she might leave him at any moment. Sometimes, when she let her guard down, he could see the sadness in her, but no matter how much he asked she wouldn't open up to him. He couldn't protect her if she didn't let him in. He shook his head, got up from the chair and left his office.

He walked to the foyer, stopping twice to speak to some of his friends. He went to the living room and mingled with the people there before going upstairs to Elena's room. He pushed the door open and walked in. The bathroom door was open and he could hear the water running. He kicked off his shoes, took his clothes off, and walked naked into the bathroom.

He got in the shower behind Elena, took the washcloth from her hands and finished washing her. Then he poured shampoo into his hand and washed her hair. She loved his hands on her. He slowly rinsed her.

When he was sure she was completely rinsed, he turned her to face him. He pulled her body tight to his and kissed her. She opened her lips for him and he pushed his tongue in. Their tongues entangled in a delicious kiss.

Elena rubbed her hips on his erection, running her hands along the back of his neck. He walked out of the stall, pulling her behind him. He took a towel and dried her, then himself. He lifted her in his arms and walked back into the room. He set her down in a standing position and embraced her.

She stroked his chest and fervidly kissed it. She circled a nipple with her tongue taking a soft nip at it then moved to the other one. She lowered her head and trailed kisses down his stomach, then she took his cock in her hand and caressed the tip with her thumb as she kept kissing him.

She moved lower until she reached his stomach. She kneeled in front of him, then moved her lips down to his cock. She flicked her tongue around the tip and played with the head for a moment before taking it into her mouth.

She twirled her tongue around the head. "Babe, that feels great," he said with a groan. She licked him from tip to base caressing him with her tongue. "Take all of me, sweetie." She opened her mouth and slowly worked her tongue around while sucking him hard. She pulled out some and then took more of him. "That's it babe."

Elena got all of him in her mouth and she sucked him hard as she fondled his sack. "I can't hold out any longer, babe. You need to let it go or I'll come in your mouth," he murmured between clenched teeth. She sucked him deeper and squeezed his sack. "Yes," he screamed as he blasted his cum into her mouth.

Elena kept sucking him, taking every bit of his cum. With his cock still semi-hard in her mouth, he grabbed her shoulders and pulled her up.

He pushed her onto the bed and climbed on top of her. He pushed her legs apart with his hands, settling between them and lowered his head to her pussy. He spread the lips apart and worked his tongue up and down, licking her as he pushed two fingers inside her. "I love the taste of your pussy," he said.

Elena gave a loud moan of approval. He kept working her pussy, licking and pushing for several minutes. His cock was hard again. He wanted to be inside her, his passion for her grew. He pulled away from her.

"Don't stop," she said between breaths.

"I want to be inside you," he said. He took her legs and pushed them up. Positioning his cock, he thrust inside her. Elena gasped for air.

Sebastian worked his cock in and out of her with hard and deep thrusts. She moved with him, swaying her hips up to meet each thrust. He grabbed her butt with his hand and pushed her higher as he lowered his head and took a nipple in his mouth. He worked the nipple, then went to the other, keeping his hips in motion.

They moved together for some time, Elena's body quivered beneath his. He knew she was ready to come so he straightened his upper body and began to thrust faster and deeper. He moved his hand to her clit and took it between his fingers and pinched it. "Ohh, ohh," she screamed as her orgasm hit her hard.

"Yes, that's it babe, come for me," he coaxed and, in seconds, he was exploding inside her. He moved against her until they both stopped shaking. He collapsed, moving to her side to avoid crushing her. He climbed out of bed and cleaned himself in the bathroom, then walked back out with a wet washcloth and cleaned her.

He wrapped an arm over her body and she shifted closer and lifted a leg over his thigh, snuggling tightly to him. Elena pressed her hand on his chest, making circles around a nipple. He lifted her face to his and took her lips for a kiss that began a second round of lovemaking.

Chapter Thirteen

Elena slowly woke up out of her nightmare. For the past few days, she had made sure to keep her nightmares a secret from Sebastian. He had persistently tried to get her to talk about them. She looked out of the window and saw that it was still daylight. She checked the time on the cable box; it was three in the afternoon.

Sebastian would be sleeping for a while longer. She removed his arm from her waist very tentatively. She climbed very slowly out of bed, grabbed the bag she had packed the night before, and quietly went to the bathroom and quickly got dressed. She stealthily made her way toward the door and picked up her jacket and shoulder bag from the corner where she left it.

She twisted the doorknob very slowly and opened the door only enough to squeeze out of the room. She stood outside the room holding the doorknob and cautiously closed it. She knew that there was no one up yet except the humans guarding the gate and one in the security room.

She moved at a steady pace down the hall and to the foyer. She opened the front door and headed for the garage. She climbed onto her favorite bike and drove off. She kept herself calm as she reached the gate. The guard came out of the gatehouse, "Hi Elena," he said to her.

Elena smiled at him. "Hi," she said.

The guard went back into the gatehouse and opened the gate for her. She drove by the gatehouse and waved to him, then sped up as she drove down the driveway. She took the road to town, driving carefully to make sure she didn't attract the attention of any vehicles driving by her.

In twenty minutes she was in town. She drove by the town hall and parked close to the library building. She shut off the bike and climbed off. She walked into the library and headed for the computer section.

She spotted an empty chair and sat down. She pulled the bag off her shoulder and took her jacket off. Taking the tablet and phone out of her bag, she started the computer, accessed her email and sent messages to James and her sister. She left her inbox open, then went into her bank accounts and transferred money around, making sure that they would have money to travel. She worked slowly, making sure to cover her tracks.

When she finished all her banking transactions, she closed her accounts and logged out. She pulled up her email inbox and checked her emails, but she still hadn't gotten a response from James or her sister. She minimized her inbox and then went through a back door into the vampire network. She pushed through the firewalls with no problem and accessed several sites, checking for any news or reports regarding the situation in Europe or anything about Sebastian.

She checked her inbox a second time with no result. She worked in the network for some time. Checking the clock on her phone, she saw that she had been there for close to two hours and she hadn't gotten a call or email.

She felt very discouraged. She had a bad feeling that something was wrong. She erased the data pertaining to this session from the hard drive and checked her email one last time. She deleted all her emails, then closed the inbox and shut down the computer. As she put her tablet inside her bag, her phone rang. She answered it right away.

"Elena."

"James. I was worried," she said.

"I'm sorry. One of Arnav's goons showed up at the market. I had to stay out front while my father talked to him. It took longer than I anticipated."

"That's okay. Is everything okay with the papers?" she asked.

"Yes, we're all set to travel in three days."

"Good. I transferred money into the account."

"Okay. Elena, I'm worried about my father. I think he's in too deep with Arnav."

"I'm so sorry."

"Never mind. I'll take care of things with Dad. I'll call you when they leave."

"Okay. James, thanks."

"Anything for you. Besides, you helped my little brother. Listen, I have to go. I'll call you. Goodbye."

"Okay, bye," she said and hung up the phone.

She put her phone in her bag, put her jacket on and threw the bag over her shoulder. She stepped away from the computer table and walked out of the library. Her nerves were wrecked; she needed more time alone before she went back to the mansion. She got on the bike and drove out of the parking lot, looking for a place to have a drink. Two blocks from downtown she found a truck-stop café. She got lucky and found a spot in front. She walked into the café, moved to the end and sat at an empty corner table.

Elena ordered a coffee and a piece of cheesecake. She sat back and pulled her phone out to check her email. Finally there was a text message from her sister. She opened it and started to read.

Hours later, Elena was still at the café. She was relieved that she had finally heard from her little sister. She had finished her piece of cheesecake long ago. She couldn't believe it when she saw that it was past two in the morning. She was so preoccupied with her family, she had lost track of time. She pulled money out her bag and put it on the table. She put on her jacket, grabbed her bag and walked out of the café. She climbed on the bike and drove off.

Elena was on the road to the mansion. She drove slowly, trying to figure out what she would tell Sebastian. She knew Sebastian was going to be angry. Twenty minutes later, she was at the gate, and the guard in the gatehouse opened the gate for her without giving her any problem. Elena passed the open gate and drove up the driveway.

Sebastian could feel the sun going down. He reached for Elena but found nothing. He opened his eyes to discover that he was alone in the room. He jumped out of bed and walked into the bathroom to find it empty too. He grabbed his pants, put them on and rushed down the stairs. He didn't bother searching for her. He walked directly into the security room and knocked on the door, finding Tom on duty. He walked into the room and Tom pulled a chair out for him. "Elena?" asked Tom.

"Yes."

"No need to watch any surveillance. I have the report from the day-time guard. She left the mansion around three, and no, she's not back yet."

"Fuck! I'm going to have to lock her in my room forever."

"Good luck with that."

"Fine, call me when she gets in. Don't bother to stop her."

"Yes, sire."

Sebastian went back to his room, took a quick shower and got dressed. He walked downstairs and went directly to Julian's office. He opened the door and walked in, but stopped short as he was confronted by the sight of Julian and Klara kissing.

Julian stopped kissing her and turned around to face his brother. "Really, do you ever knock?" Julian asked sarcastically.

"I'm glad you two are getting along so well."

"Hi Sebastian. I'll let you two talk," said Klara giving Julian a quick kiss on the lips and walking out of the office.

"Sebastian, seriously can you knock next time?" Julian requested testily as he moved behind his desk and sat down.

"Fine," he snapped back, sitting on the chair across from the desk.

Julian guessed right away that Sebastian was upset about something. "Elena?" he asked.

"Yes, she left the mansion again. She's not back yet."

"No shit. You need to put a GPS on her ass."

"No kidding."

"Well, now that you're here, I have a scheduled conference call with the team in Europe. Why don't you stay and join me?"

"Sure."

Julian picked up the receiver, clicked the speakerphone button and dialed the number.

A few hours later, Sebastian was in the living room watching a small group of his pack as they chatted. At least the call with the team in Europe went well; he was glad they decided to send the team. He sat back on his chair with a beer in his hand, content to just listen to everyone talk. He unconsciously kept twirling the beer bottle in his hand.

Sebastian pulled his phone from his pants pocket and saw that it was Tom. "Tom," he barked anxiously.

"She's on her way to the garage."

"Okay, thanks."

"No problem."

Sebastian did well keeping his temper in check. He stood up from the chair and walked to the living room doorway where he waited for her to come in. He only had to wait a few minutes before the door opened and she walked in. He moved from the doorway and met her in the foyer. "Elena. You went out again," he said.

"Hello Sebastian. Yes, I went out," she said as she tried to walk by him.

Sebastian stepped in front of her and grabbed her arm. He pulled her along with him. She tried to get away, but his hold on her was too strong. "Sebastian, please let me go," she begged.

"Please what, Elena?" he screamed at her.

Everyone heard him scream. Sebastian stood in front of her, shaking with fury. He was so tired of her keeping secrets from him. "Tell me what you want from me," he demanded, still screaming.

Elena tried to take a step away but he pulled her back. Julian moved closed to Sebastian but didn't interfere. Everyone was looking at them. "I want nothing," she yelled.

"You're mine. You can't continue to leave the mansion without telling me where you're going."

"You don't own me. I can do whatever the hell I want."

"No you can't. Go to your room," he ordered her.

"What the fuck? You can't order me around," she managed to say as he pulled her into his arms.

"Go to your room, now. Wait for me," he whispered menacingly in her ear before he let her go. Everyone in the room looked on.

Sebastian waved everyone away, then turned around and walked to his office with Julian behind him. He went to his liquor cabinet and pulled two glasses and a bottle of whiskey out of it. He sat behind his desk and motioned Julian to take one of the chairs. He poured whiskey into the glasses, gave a glass to Julian as he took the other. He gulped the whiskey in one big swallow then poured a second one. "I don't know what to do." he said.

"Maybe you should lock her in her room and throw away the key."

"Please, don't give me any ideas."

Sebastian sat back in his chair, gulped the second glass and poured another. They sat in silence drinking the whiskey.

Elena was furious with Sebastian. She frantically paced around the room in the dark. She kicked off her boots then pulled her socks off. Elena needed fresh air so she opened the balcony door. She walked out and sat down in a chair in the corner. She heard a noise below the balcony. Moving stealthily and leaning against the wall, she looked down and saw the shadows of two vampires moving to the back of the mansion.

She waited until they disappeared around a corner, then she dropped down to the ground, landing on her feet. She stayed close to the wall and followed their noisy steps, tailing them until they stopped next to what looked like an electrical box. She edged closer to them, staying in the shadows.

"Give me five minutes to get in the house. I'll set the fire in a bathroom and pull the fire alarm. Then you cut the lights. Meet me in the foyer," said the first voice, which she quickly recognized as one of the vampires from Europe.

"Okay," said the other.

Elena saw one vampire run by her and go into the house. She had no time to waste; she emerged from the shadows and moved behind the other vampire. With the force of her entire body, she slammed into him, bashing his head against the wall and knocking him unconscious. Then she turned around and ran towards the house.

Sebastian had finally decided to go face Elena. He jumped up from his chair and walked to the door as the fire alarm went off. He and Julian rushed out of the office. Everyone in the mansion was standing, looking around. Sebastian could see smoke coming from the back.

"Everybody out," he ordered. Julian rushed to where the smoke was coming from.

Elena tried the door by the kitchen but it was locked. She ran back to the terrace and tried the door of the living room, which she found open. She ran to the foyer and stopped when she saw Sebastian standing by the base of the stairs directing everyone out. She looked around for the other vampire. From the corner of her eye, she saw movement. She looked to her right and saw the vampire coming out from a corner in the family room. He was pointing a gun at Sebastian. Elena ran to him, "Sebastian," she screamed.

Sebastian turned when he heard Elena scream. She rushed to him and jumped in front of him as the vampire pulled the trigger. A shot rang out through the mansion and Elena collapsed in Sebastian's arms. At the back of the mansion Julian heard the shot and ran to the foyer in time to see Elena collapsing in Sebastian's arms. He turned around and saw two guards rush the gunman and bring him down.

"Elena!" Sebastian shouted in despair.

Julian ran to them and could see blood on Elena's back. Sebastian looked up to him with desperation on his face.

"Sebastian, let's get her to the clinic."

Sebastian turned around and rushed toward the back of the mansion where the clinic was located. Julian stayed with him as he made a call to the doctor.

"Sebastian," whispered Elena barely breathing.

"Don't talk, babe."

"The other vampire is at the back of the house."

"Babe, please," he begged her.

"My mother and sister..." she trailed off as she lost consciousness.

As they reached the clinic, the fire alarm stopped ringing. Julian opened the door and they all rushed inside. Beth, the doctor rushed to them and helped them put Elena face down on the bed. Sebastian didn't let go of her. "Sebastian, let her go, please," He stepped back but held her hand.

After snapping on a pair of gloves, Beth cut Elena's blouse apart and looked at the damage. She poked in the wound looking for the bullet. She turned to Sebastian, "This is a silver bullet. I don't know why she's still alive—she should be dead. I need to remove the bullet from her shoulder."

She went to a cabinet and pulled several medical instruments out and put them on a tray. She went to the refrigerator and got a bag of blood that she added to the tray.

"Sebastian, I need some space," she said.

Sebastian moved to the other side of the bed and held Elena's other hand. Beth rolled the tray closer to the bed and started the procedure.

"Julian, put the team in Europe on alert. Tell them to be ready for our call," he ordered.

"Okay, what about the vampires?"

"Question them, then kill them," he ordered with no hesitation.

Julian rushed out of the clinic. Sebastian stayed close to the bed. The doctor labored for more than an hour. She pulled the bullet out, stitched the wound closed and covered it up with gauze, then started an IV with the blood bag. She pulled her gloves off, threw them on the tray and pushed the tray away.

"I've done all I can. The silver bullet should have killed her. She's laboring for air, but still breathing. Help me turn her over carefully and get her comfortable." They got her in a hospital gown and covered her with the blanket.

"What else can I do?" he asked.

"Nothing. Now we wait."

CHAPTER FOURTEEN

SEBASTIAN SAT BACK IN his chair looking outside his office window in a daze. It had been three nights since the attempt on his life when Elena had been shot. She was still in critical condition and wasn't showing any signs of improvement. Sebastian was trying to remain optimistic about the situation, but he was losing hope as the days went by.

Beth, the doctor, kept telling him that she had done all she could for Elena. After she studied Elena's blood, she discovered that there was something different about it.

Sebastian turned around when he heard the door open. He looked up to see Julian walking into his office. Julian gave his brother a smile.

"Hi," Julian said sitting across from him.

"Hi," Sebastian said in a low tone.

"I've got two teams ready to go in. You just have to give the orders."

"Good," he said.

They sat in silence for some time. Sebastian was exhausted from sitting with Elena for long hours and hardly getting any sleep. He hadn't shaved in three days. He looked like a complete mess.

"Sebastian, why don't you go take a nap. I'll watch over things," Julian suggested.

"I'm fine."

Both turned their heads to the door as they heard a knock. "Come in," said Julian.

Tom opened the door and walked into the office. "My king, commander. We have a problem."

"What now?" Sebastian asked in a frustrated tone.

"A young vampire couple is at the gate asking for sanctuary."

"Again?" said Julian, "Do we look like some kind of shelter?" snapped Julian.

"My lord, the young lady says she's Elena sister."

"What?" said Sebastian, jumping up from his chair.

"My lord, she gave me this picture," said Tom handing the picture to him.

Julian moved next to Sebastian as the two looked at the picture of Elena standing with two other women.

"This is the young lady," said Tom pointing to the small girl next to his Elena.

Sebastian needed to stay calm. He took two quick breaths and looked at his little brother. "Julian, bring them to me," he said sitting back down at his desk.

Julian and Tom left the office. Sebastian pushed his hand through his unruly hair. His life was in shambles right now; he felt so alone without her. She had made him feel love for the first time in his life, and now there was a chance he could lose her. He couldn't accept that.

Minutes later, Julian and Tom walked into the office with two young people behind them. Sebastian knew right away that the young lady was Elena's little sister. Her eyes had the same warmth.

"My king," said the young man, bowing his head. "I'm Matt." Sebastian didn't pay any attention to him; he kept his eyes on the young lady. He could see her big sister's defiance in her eyes. "Where is my sister?" Ayla asked firmly.

"Ayla," said Matt pulling her to him.

Sebastian looked at both of them and saw the bond that was between them. He remained silent, just staring at them.

"I want to see my sister," she snapped, then softened her tone, "please."

"Sit," he ordered.

Matt took Ayla's hand and pulled her to a chair, then sat down next to her.

Julian moved from behind his desk while Tom remained behind the couple. Sebastian waited for a few seconds before speaking to them. "What's your name?" he asked the girl.

"My name is Ayla," she answered.

"Last name."

"Steward."

Sebastian looked at Julian.

"Why the different last name?" asked Julian.

Ayla looked at him, then at Matt, hesitating. She finally said, "It's a long story."

"We have time. Tell us."

"I can't. It's not my story to tell; it's Elena's."

"Tell me," Sebastian ordered slamming his hand on the desk staring into her eyes.

Ayla was petrified of him but didn't flinch. She stared back at him in silence.

"Ayla," said Matt, taking her hand in his, "Tell him, my love," he said kissing her hand.

"Fine," she said, "you two may want to sit down."

Tom and Julian sat down next to her. She sat back in her chair and began the story.

Ayla told them about the death of their father and how, after his death, Elena moved them away and changed her name. She related the steps Elena took to protect them from their leader. After the leader's death, his son Arnav took over and Ayla explained how Arnav was worse than his father. When Arnav met Elena at an event she had planned, he became obsessed with her.

Ayla told them that when Arnav found out that Elena was going to be the ceremony planner for the king's mating ceremony, he approached her with the assassination job. She assured them that Elena refused the job, but after several months he came back to her, telling her that he knew about her hidden family. She related how Arnav threatened Elena with their lives if she didn't accept the job.

Ayla stopped talking for a moment. Matt caressed her hand and smiled at her encouragingly. She continued with her story, telling them that Elena took the job, but Ayla assured them that Elena never had any intention of killing the king and that immediately after she accepted the job, they knew that Arnav had put a surveillance team on them. That's when Elena came up with the plan to get them out of Russia and bring them to Louisiana where she hoped the king would protect them. With the help of Elena's best friend James, they got the papers started. James requested to get Matt out as well.

Ayla told them that she believed that Elena never intended to stay in Louisiana; she suspected that her intention was to go back to Russia and kill Arnav. She said that Elena told her several times that Arnav would never stop going after her—he wanted her. Ayla stopped talking as Matt pulled her closer and gave her a quick kiss on the lips.

Sebastian, Julian and Tom listened quietly to all that Ayla told them. When she was finished, Sebastian stood up and paced behind his desk. He stopped his pacing and looked at Ayla, "Where is your mother?" he asked.

Tears ran down Ayla's cheeks but she didn't say anything.

"Arnav's men got to her before we could get her out," said Matt in a voice filled with sadness.

"Julian, have the teams move in on Arnav. Distribute the picture of Elena's mother to them. Tell them to find her and get her to safety. That's their priority," he said firmly. He turned back to Ayla, "What's your mother's name?" he asked.

"Iskra."

"Tom, double the security. Tell everyone to stay alert."

Julian and Tom nodded to him and left the office. Sebastian turned his attention back to the young couple. "Can I see my sister?" asked Ayla.

Sebastian's expression changed to one of intense emotional pain. "What's wrong with my sister?" she asked.

Sebastian moved next to her. "Ayla, your sister has been shot. She's been unconscious for three days. Our doctor doesn't know what to do," he said.

Ayla jumped out of her chair, "I know! She needs my blood."

"Why?" She hesitated. "Ayla, why," he demanded.

She looked at Matt who nodded his head. "We have Fae blood in our system. My father was a Fae."

"Of course," Sebastian said slamming his hand on the back of the chair, "That's why you can go out in the daylight."

"Yes, we can't stay out the whole day, but we can move for a while. Please bring me to her. I can help her."

"Follow me," he said walking out of the office.

Ayla and Matt walked behind Sebastian, keeping pace with him. Julian met them down the hall.

"We're all set with the teams. They'll call me when they're going in."

"Good."

Sebastian opened the door to the clinic and walked in with the other three behind him. Ayla saw her sister on the bed and rushed past Sebastian. "Elena," she screamed with tears rolling down her face. She turned back to Sebastian and the others, "What's wrong with her?" she asked.

"She was shot with a silver bullet," answered Beth, emerging from a small office.

"Oh my God," Ayla said, as more tears came down. Matt embraced her and Ayla leaned her head on his chest.

"You said you can help her," Sebastian said.

"Yes," she said looking up at him. "My blood will help. We need to do a transfusion."

"Your blood is different," Beth stated, now standing by the bed.

"Yes, we're half Fae."

"I knew it. Oh my God, yes, that will definitely help her."

Beth quickly moved to the cabinet and pulled out all the necessary instruments to perform the transfusion.

"Julian, bring a bed and put it next to Elena's. What's your name?" she asked turning to Ayla.

"Ayla."

"Ayla, take your clothes off and put a gown on. There are lockers through that door," she pointed to the left.

Ayla gave Matt her backpack and hurried to the lockers as Julian brought in the bed. Matt moved to the side, watching the doctor organize a tray. Ayla walked back into the room.

"Lay down," Beth directed as she moved between the beds and finished setting up. She put her gloves on, then worked quietly as they all watched. By this time, Sebastian was at the other side of the bed holding Elena's hand. Julian and Matt hung back, trying to stay out of the way. After several minutes, Beth finished the transfusion. She pulled her gloves off and looked at Ayla. "All set. Do you need anything?" she asked.

"No, I'm fine."

Beth pushed the tray away then moved from in between the beds. "Now we wait," she said to Sebastian anticipating his question before he asked it and patting him on the back.

She rolled the tray away and went to the back room to clean the instruments. They remained silent for several minutes.

"I have to go," Sebastian said to Ayla. "I'll be back as soon as I can."

"Me too," said Julian.

Sebastian kissed Elena's hand and walked out with Julian.

Matt pulled a chair next to Ayla's bed and sat down. He took her hand in his and smiled at her. He sat quietly, keeping watch over her as she closed her eyes to get some rest. An hour later, Beth came out of her office. Ayla heard her coming and opened her eyes. "I'm going out for a moment. I'll be back as soon as I can."

"Take your time. We'll stay here with her," said Ayla.

"You're sure?"

"Yes."

"Call me if anything changes. My phone number is under the phone, okay?"

"Okay," said Matt and Ayla in unison.

Beth walked out of the clinic. "She's gone," Ayla said.

"About time," said Elena, opening her eyes. "Hi sis," she said smiling.

"Hi," Ayla said.

"Where's Mom?" she asked.

Ayla put her head down and tears rolled down her face, but she said nothing.

"I'm sorry Elena. They got to her before we could get her out," said Matt.

"It's not your fault. I'll get her out. Get me two bandages," she said.

Matt went to the cabinet, found the bandages and brought them to her. "Grab some chairs and put them under the doorknobs, lock them too," she said pulling the needle from her arm and putting a bandage on it.

Elena stood up, stopped the dripping from the transfusion tubes, then went and pulled out her sister's needle. She put the bandage on her sister's arm and they hugged. Matt did as Elena requested and went back to stand next to Ayla's bed. Elena pulled away from her sister. "Listen to me. Stay here for as long as you can. Don't let anyone in. Let them break the door down. I need as much time as possible to get out of here."

"Elena."

"I'll get Mom out. Sebastian will take care of you, okay? Matt, give me one of your shirts."

Matt pulled a shirt out of his backpack and gave it to her. Elena pulled her hospital gown off and put the shirt on. She gave each of them a kiss on the forehead and moved to the back door.

"Elena be careful," said Ayla.

"I will. Matt, watch over her. She's your responsibility."

"Yes, I'll guard her with my life."

Elena smiled at them, pulling the chair from under the doorknob. "Matt put the chair back after I've gone. See you soon," she said walking out of the clinic.

Matt followed her directions, walked back to Ayla's bed, and grabbed her hand. Ayla wrapped her hands around his and smiled at him.

CHAPTER FIFTEEN

ELENA MOVED SWIFTLY AND quietly down the hall. She climbed the back stairs and reached her bedroom. She dressed quickly and put on her socks and boots. She found her bag and checked to make sure everything was there. She went to the closet and, from a secret compartment in one of her bags, she pulled out a new ID, passport and credit cards. She stuffed everything into her bag and walked out of the room.

She took the back stairs again, this time walking down to the garage. Instead of taking the bike, she climbed into a sedan and pulled out of the garage and down the driveway. She stopped at the gate and could see that there was more security than usual. She slowed down her breath and smiled to the guard who smiled back at her and opened the gate.

Elena waved to him as she drove through the gate. She kept her speed slow, trying not to attract any unnecessary attention. She pulled out of the driveway and onto the main road. In minutes, she was on the highway at which point she accelerated. She needed to get as far from the mansion as possible. After a short drive, Elena took the exit for the small airport.

She parked the car in the parking lot, left the keys in the ignition and walked into the airport building. She bought a ticket to Kansas, where she would connect to Europe. She didn't have to wait long before she boarded the plane. She checked the time on her cell phone. She hoped that Matt and Ayla had not been discovered yet. Minutes later, the plane was in the air.

Elena pulled her tablet out, went to the airline website and bought a ticket from Kansas to London with a transfer from London to Russia. She paid for the ticket and shut off her tablet. She leaned her head back. Her shoulder was aching, but she couldn't afford to dwell on the pain. She closed her eyes but stayed alert. The flight from Texas to Kansas was a little more than an hour, so she took the time to review her plan to get her mother away from Arnav and out of Europe.

The plane made it to Kansas in good time, but she still barely had time to run through the terminal and get to her departure gate. She made it to the gate to find that passengers were already boarding. Her section hadn't been called yet, so she sat down to catch her breath. When her section was called a few minutes later, she boarded the plane, settled back in her seat and buckled the seatbelt. Twenty minutes later, she was in the air again on her way to London.

Sebastian was in his office when someone knocked loudly at the door. "Come in," he said.

It was the doctor and she seemed upset. "We've got a problem," Beth said as she swiftly crossed the room and stood in front of his desk.

"Elena?" he asked angrily.

"I don't know. The door is locked. I knocked but no one will answer," she said.

Sebastian and Julian ran out of the office with Beth behind them. When they reached the clinic, Sebastian tried the door with no luck.

"Here's my key," Beth said, handing it to him.

He unlocked the door and the knob turned but still the door didn't open. He knocked hard on the door and got no answer. "Matt, Ayla, open the door," he yelled.

Infuriated, he shoved his shoulder against the door, which instantly broke at the hinges. All three rushed into the room.

The doctor rushed to the beds, which were empty. Sebastian looked around the room and saw Matt and Ayla in each other's arms against the wall. Sebastian rushed over to them and Matt moved Ayla behind him and took a fighting stance.

"Don't you touch her," he snapped.

"What the fuck?" said Julian grabbing Sebastian's arm. "Listen we're not going to hurt anyone, okay," he said calmly.

Sebastian stood beside his brother, his body trembling. "Where is Elena?"

"She left," Ayla showed her head from behind Matt.

"Where did she go?"

"She went to get Mom," she answered.

"Arrggh, stubborn woman!"

"Tell me about it. I've got one too," said Matt.

"How long ago? Did she say what airport?"

"Over two hours. No, she didn't," Ayla answered.

"Damn it. Doc, get these two in a room. Order the plane to get ready. We have to leave right away," he said facing Julian.

"I'm going with you," Julian said, pulling his phone out and making the necessary calls.

"I'm going too," said Ayla.

"No, you just stay here," Sebastian ordered. "If you can't control her, I'll have her locked in a cell," he said to Matt.

"I've got her," Matt said firmly.

"Good," Sebastian said turning and walking out of the clinic.

Julian followed him while giving orders over the phone. They got to Sebastian's office where he got their passports out of the safe. He checked for his phone in his pocket then threw Julian's passport to him. They walked out of the office and into the foyer. Sebastian was so worried about Elena that he couldn't speak.

Beth waited for a few minutes, then walked Matt and Ayla up the stairs and into a room. "I suggest you stay here," she said turning around and leaving them alone in the room.

Ayla held tight to Matt and started to cry. "She'll be fine. She's smart and strong, okay?" Matt said.

Ayla nodded her head, not saying anything. Matt walked her to a sofa and sat down lifting her onto his lap. He kissed her head and wrapped his arms tightly around her.

Elena checked the time; she still had about six hours before she got to London. She pulled her phone out and sent a text message to her sister then shut it off and kept it in her hand. She rested her head and closed her eyes to get some rest. Several minutes later, her phone vibrated. She opened it and read Ayla's reply.

Elena took a deep breath and sent another text back. She knew that there was a good chance that Sebastian would catch up with her or even get there before her, but she had an advantage over him. She had James on alert to pick her up at the airport and she knew Arnav would be hiding far from the compound, and she knew where to find him.

Sebastian and Julian with a third team were already in the air. Julian was talking with the team leader on the phone. After several minutes he hung up.

"The teams took over the compound, but so far there's no sign of Arnav or Elena's mother. They still have a section of the compound to search. They will call with a progress report as soon as they can."

"Motherfucker, I'm going to tear him apart," Sebastian said angrily. It was good that it would be dark when they reached London, but they knew it would be close to dawn by the time they got to Russia.

Sebastian sat back in his seat and closed his eyes. The fact that the woman he loved had to sacrifice so much was tearing him apart. They should have kept a closer eye on the European pack, but he was so wrapped up in keeping the peace between the packs and managing all the bullshit politics with the humans that he didn't see it. Now Elena was hurting and probably in danger. He was supposed to protect her. He banged his elbow hard on the back of his seat. "Damn it," he said out loud.

The others all kept their heads down, not wanting to upset Sebastian further. Julian saw that Sebastian's temper was flaring and he didn't blame him. He had gotten close to Klara and knew he would kill anyone who threatened her. Sebastian stirred in his chair. "You've gotten close to Klara. What would you do if she was in danger?" Sebastian asked his brother.

"I'd kill anyone who threatened her. But listen Bash, she's going to be fine. She's strong," Julian said touching his arm.

"We should have known what was going on in Europe," Sebastian said with his eyes closed.

"Don't blame yourself," Julian said.

"Who should I blame, you? I'm the king, I'm supposed to know this stuff," he snapped.

"Sebastian, give yourself a break. You've been busy with other things."

Sebastian turned to look into his brother's eyes, "She's my woman. I'm supposed to protect her. She's alone."

Julian moved back in his seat and didn't say anything else. Sebastian closed his eyes again and went back to thinking about her.

Elena was already on the flight to Russia. She spent the entire flight to London and now the flight to Russia working on a plan to get into Arnav's hideout. She still had another two hours before she arrived in Russia. She put her seat back, closed her eyes and tried to rest for the remainder of the flight.

When Elena's plane had landed, she stood up quickly and waited for them to open the door. She impatiently watched the people in the rows in front of her walking off of the plane. Gripping her shoulder bag tightly, she waited for the passenger next to her to move into the aisle and she followed close behind. She separated from the crowd as soon as she could, rushed out of the airport and stood in a corner watching for James. She heard the sound of a bike approaching. She emerged from her corner, hoping it was James. He pulled up right in front of her. They didn't have time for pleasantries—he handed her a helmet and she climbed on the back, wrapping her arms around him.

James drove about twenty minutes then slowed down and drove into an alleyway behind his friend's bar. He drove to the end and found a dark corner and parked the bike. They climbed off the bike and took off their helmets.

Elena rushed into his already open arms for a long hug. James gave her a quick kiss on her lips before taking her hand and leading her to the back door of the bar. James inserted the key in the door and opened it. He directed her to a back room, and James took out a bottle of water from the small refrigerator and gave it to her. He pulled out a chair for Elena and she sat down. He sat down next to her. "Okay, so how are we getting in?" he asked.

Elena pulled her tablet out of her bag. She opened the map of a small warehouse she had previously downloaded from the town hall property records. Together they looked over the schematics and decided the best way to get in and out of the warehouse. Elena sat back and drank some of the water. "Let's go," she said putting the bottle down on the small table.

James grabbed her hand and together they walked out of the room and back outside. Quickly, they climbed on the bike and James drove off.

The plane that was carrying Sebastian and his team was now on its way to Russia. Sebastian kept his eyes closed for the entire trip. No one spoke to him, including Julian. Sebastian opened his eyes when he heard the airplane intercom go on. He listened to the pilot announce that they were twenty minutes from Russia and would begin to descend. Everyone straightened in their seats and buckled their seatbelts.

When Sebastian's plane landed, the exited the plane. Sebastian stayed back as everyone disembarked. He picked up the bag with his weapons and walked off the plane with Julian. The team was on the ground waiting for them. They all climbed into two large SUVs, and the driver took off.

In the SUV, Sebastian contemplated the situation, still wondering what he could have done to help the European pack. After about thirty minutes of driving, they reached their destination. The teams rushed out of the SUVs and the commander in charge of the mission approached Sebastian and Julian. "My king, commander, we have searched the entire compound and Arnav and Elena's mother are not on site," he said.

"Impossible," snapped Sebastian.

"Sire, we've been questioning the vampires who are loyal to Arnav, and we have confirmation that he was here, and the lady too, but somehow they escaped the compound. We're still questioning others, but we have no more information right now."

"Fuck. Bring me to the prisoners," Sebastian yelled.

"This way," said the commander.

The commander walked alongside Sebastian and guided him to one of the smaller buildings. They walked in and Sebastian strode over to the group being guarded in the corner. He looked at the faces of everyone gathered and slowly circled the group for several minutes.

"Bring me those three," he ordered, pointing to three vampires who kept themselves apart from the group.

The commander relayed his order and quickly the guards pulled the three vampires away and brought them to a separate room.

Chapter Sixteen

James drove into the industrial park and parked the bike in a dark spot at the back of the first warehouse. Elena got off the bike and stretched her legs. They took off their helmets and James placed them on top of the bike.

Elena took the lead as they moved slowly and quietly toward the back of the building, keeping to the shadows. Elena moved at a steady but cautious pace. Suddenly, Elena signaled James to stop. From their dark hiding spot, she could see the lights on the third floor of Arnav's warehouse.

They moved along the wall, hugging it tight. They rushed across, reaching the back of the building next to Arnav's warehouse. Elena saw two vampires guarding the back door. She pointed at James to stay put. She was glad she did her research on the buildings that surrounded the leader's warehouse.

Elena dropped her bag in a corner, moved next to the building and slowly climbed the fire escape ladder. She reached the roof and pulled two large daggers from behind her back. From her vantage point, she could clearly see the vampires guarding Arnav's building.

Sebastian and Julian, together with the commander, finished questioning the last of the three vampires. Satisfied with their findings all three walked out of the room.

"We need a map of the industrial park," said Julian.

The commander pulled out various rolled-up maps of the area and put them on a large table. Sebastian and Julian stood at each side of the table while the commander rolled out the maps one at a time. The third map was the one they were looking for.

They located the warehouse that Arnav owned and studied the schematics of the building and established a plan of attack. Based on the information they collected from the three vampires, Arnav escaped with only a handful of vampires. With the plan established, everyone got ready to go.

Sebastian gave the order for a team to stay at the compound. The other two teams prepared their weapons and piled into the SUVs. They input the warehouse address in the GPS of the lead SUV where Sebastian was sitting. Julian was in the second SUV. The vehicles raced out of the compound.

Back at the industrial park, Elena was kneeling on the roof waiting for the right moment to jump the vampires. She only had to wait a few minutes. The two vampires stood next to each other in idle conversation. With her vampire speed and strength, she pushed off the building roof with the daggers in her hands, landing behind the vampires. Swiftly, she slit their throats before they had the chance to call out, and with one clean slash, she severed their heads from their bodies. The vampires instantly disintegrated in front of her.

James appeared next to her and slowly she opened the door. She signaled James to stay behind her, and quietly they climbed the stairs two at a time.

The SUV carrying Sebastian and his team took the turn into the industrial park. They stopped at a safe distance and Sebastian quickly jumped out of the SUV followed by the rest of the group.

"Team A will take the front and Team B the back. I'm with Team A. I'll signal when to go in," barked the commander.

With his team behind him, Sebastian ran to the alley between the buildings. They reached the back and slowly worked their way behind Arnav's warehouse. Sebastian signaled for everyone to stop when he could see the back entrance. He was surprised it wasn't being guarded. He signaled for two guards to scout the area. They were back in less than five minutes. "There were two guards in the back," said one of the men in a low voice.

"Where are they now?" asked Sebastian in a harsh whisper.

"Dead. Their ashes are on the top of the stairs. We found this by the corner of the other building," said the other guard handing him the bag.

"Fuck, it's Elena. She's already here," growled Sebastian.

"Ready in front," the commander informed Sebastian over the headphone.

"Ready here. Be advised that Elena is already in the building," he said.

"On five, it's 3:30 right now."

"Correct," said Sebastian.

Inside the building, Elena killed another vampire on the second floor staircase. She and James were moving swiftly to the third floor. She could sense another vampire close by and signaled for James to stop. Elena kept climbing and located the vampire hiding behind a corner wall at the top of the stairway. She climbed two more stairs, then jumped to the railing at the base of the stairway and flipped over it, pulling a dagger from her back. At an amazing speed, she jumped the vampire, grabbing the back of his neck, slammed him against the wall and slashed his throat.

She stepped away from the body and watched it turn to ashes. James ran up to her and slowly, she opened the door. She looked down both sides of the hall and found no one in sight. She signaled James to come in and together they moved quietly to the front of the building where she had seen the lights from the street.

When they reached the door, Elena pulled the other dagger out. They walked through the door and moved towards the voices. From behind a pile of boxes stacked to the roof, Elena could hear Arnav talking to another vampire. In the corner she saw her mother tied to a chair.

She pulled James aside and whispered in his ear, "I'm going in. Go to my mom and get her out. I'll take care of the other vampire and Arnav."

James nodded in agreement. They stepped closer to the boxes. Elena rushed the other vampire first, swiftly going for his throat and puncturing it. Arnav saw her launch from behind the stack of boxes and jump the other vampire. He pulled his knife out and ran to them, but by the time he got there she had cut off the vampire's head.

James reached Elena's mom and quickly cut the ropes tied around her arms and legs. He pulled the gag from her mouth. Iskra stood up with shaky legs. He wrapped an arm around her waist to steady her and hurried out. He didn't like leaving Elena alone with Arnav, but she made him promise to get her mother to safety. He and Iskra reached the door, but before he opened it, he looked back towards Elena. He saw Arnav and Elena facing each other with daggers in hand. He turned around, opened the door and stepped out into the hall and ran down the stairs, all the while keeping a tight hold on Iskra.

They made it to the second floor stairs, but when they got there a team of vampires surrounded them. James stopped. One of the vampires who he assumed was the leader stepped in front of him. "Stop. That's Elena's mother. Who are you?" Sebastian asked.

"I'm James," he answered.

"You two, search the second floor," he said pointing to two guards. "You stay with them," he said to another one.

"Where is Elena?" he asked.

"She's on the third floor fighting Arnav," answered James.

"Damn it. Let's go," he said running up the stairs.

Sebastian reached the third floor with the three remaining guards ran behind him. He opened the door and rushed in. As he reached the area where he could hear fighting going on, Julian's team entered behind them.

Elena rapidly swung a dagger across her body, catching Arnav on the bicep. Arnav quickly pulled back from her then positioned himself to face her. For a short time, they fought hard and fast. Elena moved sideways avoiding some of his slashes but she still had many cuts everywhere on her body, including a deep cut on her thigh that severely slowed her down.

She sidestepped him with a counter move then jumped at him. Arnav caught her in midair and flipped her on the floor ending up on top of her. Elena kicked him off her and rolled away, standing up to face him again.

Elena saw movement from the corner of her eye, which distracted her briefly. Arnav had seen Sebastian and the others come in and used Elena's distraction to his advantage. He quickly turned her around and grabbed her by her throat, forcefully slamming her back against his chest. He tightened his hold on her, then pressed the dagger against her throat.

The two teams reached the area and surrounded them. Arnav stepped back, dragging her with him.

"Arnav, stop!" Sebastian yelled.

"Well, who have we here? The mighty Sebastian, King of the Vampires," he said sarcastically.

"Let her go."

"No can do. Don't take another step or I'll cut off her head."

"Nobody move," ordered Sebastian.

Elena looked at Sebastian aware that there was blood dripping down her face. She struggled with Arnav's chokehold. "Kill him," she yelled.

"You move, she dies," Arnav warned Sebastian.

"Don't listen to him; he's going to kill me anyway," she yelled.

"Elena, you wound my heart," he said mocking her.

"Fuck you, Arnav," she said as she lifted her foot surreptitiously, trying to reach in her boot for her small knife.

"That's not the way to talk to me, honey," he said tightening the dagger against her throat.

The team watched as Elena reached for the knife. "You better kill me now because you'll never get out of here alive," she yelled as she pulled the knife out and launched it into the forearm that was holding the dagger.

As Elena shoved the knife into Arnav's arm, Sebastian lunged forward, while, at the same time, Arnav dropped the dagger and loosened his hold on Elena. Her body collapsed on the floor as Sebastian grabbed Arnav by the throat and swiftly slashed his head off.

Sebastian dropped Arnav's head and rushed to Elena who was unconscious on the floor. He dropped to his knees next to her. Arnav's body was nothing but a pile of ashes. Everyone surrounded Sebastian and Elena.

"Elena, babe," he murmured folding her body in his arms. "Elena, babe," he said again.

Julian moved close to him and touched his shoulder, "Sebastian we need to get out of here. The commander informed me that the police are on their way," he said.

"Get everyone out. She's going to need medical attention," he said standing with her in his arms.

One part of the team swiftly moved in front of him and the other moved to cover his back. Together they rushed down the stairs and out of the building. Sebastian climbed into the first SUV, the rest of the team hopped into the others. "She needs a doctor," he said as they drove out of the industrial park.

"My lord, we have a medic at the compound. I'll call ahead. We'll be there in twenty minutes," said the commander.

"Make it faster," ordered Sebastian.

The SUV flew past the empty streets because it was early in the morning. They reached the compound in fifteen minutes and drove directly to the building where the clinic was located.

As soon as they stopped the SUV, Sebastian jumped out and rushed into the clinic. A guard held the door open for him and the medic met him in the front hall with a gurney. Sebastian settled Elena on the gurney and he and the medic rolled her into the examination room.

"My lord, I need space," the medic said.

Sebastian stepped back as the medic rolled a tray with medical instruments over to the gurney. Quickly, he cut off her clothes and cleaned the blood off to see the extent of her wounds. After a few minutes he had completed the examination. He walked over to Sebastian who had been standing against the wall during the examination.

"My lord, most of the wounds are superficial, but there are several that will need stitches. She's lost a lot of blood. We need to give her a transfusion."

Sebastian nodded his head and moved next to the bed to hold her hand. The medic got the needle to stitch her up and pulled blood from the refrigerator.

Julian spoke to James and Iskra, then pulled his phone out and called Klara. He let her know about the situation and what was happening with Elena. He asked her to pass the word to Ayla and Matt. He spoke a few minutes more with Klara then hung up the phone.

It took the medic another hour to stitch Elena's wounds and then he set up an IV for her. He got her comfortable in the bed and covered her body. "She has a lot of healing to do. It may be awhile before she wakes up," he said.

"Thanks," said Sebastian pulling a chair close to the bed and sitting down.

Sebastian, Julian and the teams restored order in the European pack. They were now without a leader, but Sebastian promised the pack he would find a replacement soon. He held several meetings with them and informed them of the situation. He assured them that they had his complete support. The pack expressed their gratitude to him.

For two days, Sebastian was busy with the meetings, but half of the time, his focus was on Elena. She was awake now but still hurting. She didn't say anything to him about the shooting and the fight in the warehouse and he didn't push her to talk.

Sebastian didn't like the way she shut him out of her life. It was as if she put up a wall between them and he didn't know how to bring it down. He could see how happy she was when James and her mother were around, but as soon as he got close to her, she changed.

Elena never thought that loving someone could hurt so much. She hoped that pushing Sebastian away would stop the pain. She wasn't willing to accept being second in his life or even his mistress. Now they were ready to leave Europe. Elena closed her eyes and a tear rolled down her cheek, which she quickly brushed off. She pulled her jacket on, grabbed her shoulder bag and left the clinic.

She walked over to the teams that were gathered around the SUVs. She saw Sebastian coming out of the main building with the commander. He shook hands with him and the commander stood back as Sebastian walked to the SUVs. She knew from James that Sebastian was leaving a team behind to keep order in the pack.

Elena stepped back and walked to the last SUV and stood behind two large guards. Sebastian looked for her and saw her standing behind the guards, which made him furious, but he said nothing. "Let's go," he ordered.

Everyone climbed in an SUV. Elena saw James and Iskra getting in one, so she got in the SUV next to her mother. None of the guards said anything to her. Elena knew they had a thirty-minute drive to the airport so she settled her head back on the seat and closed her eyes.

Just as expected, they reached the airport in thirty minutes. Elena opened her eyes when the SUV stopped and she climbed out behind one of the guards. She pulled her bag over her shoulder and followed the group. As she was waiting in line to board the plane, she felt a hand on her waist; she knew it was Sebastian. It felt so good to be held by him. Sebastian moved beside her and wrapped his arm around her waist. She leaned her body into his.

When they had finally boarded the plane, he directed her to the front where two seats were available for them. Sebastian and Elena settled into their seats, buckled their seatbelts and, within twenty minutes, the plane took off. Sebastian pulled up the armrest between them and Elena scooted closer to him. Sebastian wrapped his arm over her shoulder; she rested her head on his chest and closed her eyes. Sebastian closed his eyes and leaned his head back on the seat, happy to have her next to him.

After six hours of flying, the plane had to stop to refuel. While the plane was fueling up, Elena took the chance to stretch her legs and went to the bathroom. When she came back, Sebastian wasn't in his seat. She settled back in her chair, pulled her phone out and checked her messages. She had one from her sister, so she responded and shut off the phone.

A few minutes later, Sebastian came back and sat next to her. He pulled her onto his lap and gave her a kiss. Elena wrapped her arms around his neck and opened her mouth for him. Sebastian launched his tongue into her mouth. They were kissing for a while when Julian walked from the back of the plane to find Sebastian and Elena kissing. "Really? Couldn't you two wait until we get home," he said loudly.

Sebastian stopped kissing her and looked up at his brother and gave him the finger. Julian responded with a big grin. Elena wiggled out of Sebastian's lap and went back to her seat. She straightened her clothes, settled back in and buckled up. She saw Sebastian gave his brother a hard look and Julian shrug his shoulders.

Minutes later, the plane took off for a second time. Elena turned her face away from Sebastian and closed her eyes. She knew she shouldn't let him kiss her, but it felt so good to be in his arms again.

Sebastian started a discussion with Julian about the steps needed to get the European pack reorganized. After agreeing on several points, Julian wrote down some notes on his tablet. They finished the discussion and Julian shut down his tablet.

Elena was aware of Sebastian resting quietly beside her for the rest of the flight, while the others in the group did the same or talked softly. Elena tried to sleep but she couldn't stop thinking about the fact that Sebastian was getting mated in less than two weeks. She was feeling sad again but she knew that the truth was that she had not expected to live through this assignment, and she certainly hadn't expected to fall in love, especially with a king.

Elena managed to take a small nap and she woke up when she felt someone shaking her. Elena opened her eyes to see Julian standing in front of her. "We've landed," he said.

Elena unbuckled her seatbelt, grabbed her bag from her lap and pulled it over her shoulder. Julian let her walk in front of him. She got off the plane and went straight to the last SUV.

She didn't talk to anyone in the SUV, but looked out the window during the entire drive. The trip to the mansion was short; in no time they were at the front gate. The guard opened the gate and the SUVs started to move again. She watched as the mansion came into view. As soon as the SUV stopped, she jumped out of it.

Sebastian climbed out of the SUV and followed her inside. "Elena," he called.

Elena ignored him and continued walking. The others in the team moved through the foyer.

"Elena," Sebastian said, reaching for her and grabbing her arm.

"What?" she snapped.

The few people still in the foyer turned around to look at them. "Where are you going?" he asked.

"To my room," she answered stepping away from him.

"I ordered your things to be moved to my room."

Elena turned to face him, "Why the hell did you do that? You have no right," she yelled.

"I do have the right; you're my woman."

Elena stepped up and confronted him, "You don't own me."

"I'm your king. You will do as I say," he screamed.

Elena's face dropped. She was very angry with him but she didn't know what to say. She looked around the foyer and saw that everyone's eyes were on her. She stepped back and lowered her eyes to the floor. "Yes, my king," she said quietly in an even tone. "May I go now?" she asked, not looking at him.

"Yes," he answered.

Elena turned around and rushed up the stairs. She moved down the hall towards Sebastian's room.

Inside Sebastian's bedroom, Elena was in the bathroom undressing. She walked into the stall and started the water. Her hands were shaking as she picked up the washcloth and soap—that's how mad she was at him. She washed herself as she tried hard to calm down. She could feel the beginning of a headache coming on. Her mind was in turmoil. She finished showering, shut off the water and walked out of the stall. She quickly dried off, wrapped the towel around her body and walked back into the room.

She didn't have the energy to face him so she turned off the light. She didn't even bother to put any clothes on. She walked to the side of the bed that faced the balcony sliding door, dropped the towel on the floor and slid into bed. She only pulled the blanket up to her lower body. She closed her eyes and hoped she would fall asleep before he came in.

CHAPTER SEVENTEEN

SEBASTIAN HAD BEEN MISERABLE for the past few days. He was busy conferencing every day with the commander in Europe, making sure everything was going well there. On top of that, Elena and he had barely spoken to each other since they got back. She kept her distance from him. The only people she talked to were her family and friends. She had a close relationship with James, which he didn't like.

Elena spent most of her days training for long hours. Sebastian didn't join her any longer. She also helped her mother to join groups and got her to participate in activities, with the hope she'd find an interest in a specific job. The rest of the time, she roamed around the mansion avoiding Sebastian. She knew he kept a close eye on her.

She walked out of the house and took a short walk in the garden before she sat down on a corner bench. She couldn't believe that there were only two days left until the ceremony. She was still on top of all the preparations and everything was running smoothly. Klara was completely thrilled with the job she was doing.

With the ceremony approaching, Elena was planning how and when to leave the mansion and walk away from the man she loved. She shook her head; for a moment she felt the pain in her heart again. Tears fell down her cheeks. She quickly wiped them away and got up to walk around again.

Sebastian sat on his chair deep in thought, wondering what he could possibly do to get closer to Elena. She had been so distant since they got back. He wanted to give her some space, but he also wanted to be with her. He was so involved with his thoughts that he didn't hear the knock on the door.

Sebastian lifted his head when Julian opened the door and walked in with James behind him. "I'm sorry," Sebastian said, "I didn't hear you knock."

"That's okay."

"Please sit down," he said to both men pointing to the chairs.

Julian and James walked to the front of the desk and sat down.

"James, how are you doing?" he asked.

"Good."

"Julian has mentioned that you would like to go back home."

"Yes, I love it here, but my life and parents are still there."

"I understand. James, I have a proposition for you," he said.

"Really?"

"Yes. Julian and I have discussed this at length. Julian has agreed to become the leader of the European pack."

"That's great news," James said.

"We also agreed that you would be perfect as the head of security for the pack. I have decided to give you the position."

"My king, I'm so honored."

Sebastian and Julian looked at each other with smiles on their faces. "So that means you'll take the position?"

"Yes, I will," he said.

"Great," Sebastian said standing up and stretching his hand out to him.

James stood up from his chair and shook Sebastian's hand then Julian's. Sebastian and Julian went over the job description and salary in detail. Julian gave several documents to James to be signed and returned to him. After they finished their discussion, Sebastian decided to ask James about Elena. "James, you've been Elena's friend for a long time," he began.

"Yes, we've been friends since preschool."

"That long?" Julian said.

"Elena once saved me from being punched by a bully and then she decided that she would become by protector. Since that time, we've been friends."

Sebastian was silent for a moment before he spoke again, "You've also been more than friends."

"Yes," was all that James said. "If you want to know more, you should ask her."

Julian stood up and said, "We should leave you alone."

James got up and they both walked towards the door. James turned around and looked at Sebastian, "She would never accept being second. She would leave you first."

Sebastian stood up from his chair and walked over to him. "She's mine, I'll take care of her."

James smiled at him and walked out of the office behind Julian. Sebastian ran his hand over his face and took a deep breath. He walked out of his office and went to meet with Klara.

Elena saw Sebastian coming from the other hall and hid in the corner. She watched as he walked into Klara's bedroom. She brought her hand to her mouth to stop anyone from hearing the sobs that came out. She rushed into her room and walked out onto the balcony. She gripped the railing hard and quickly jumped down, then ran at vampire speed into the woods. She didn't stop running until she reached the area she recognized. She sat down under a tree, leaned her head back against it and let her tears pour down. She lay down on the grass, rested her head on her arm and closed her eyes. She lay there crying for a long time.

After Sebastian finished talking to Klara he went down and joined Julian for a game of pool. He played a couple of games before he saw James, Matt and Ayla walk in the room.

He approached them then said, "Hi, have you seen Elena?"

"No," they all said.

"Maybe she's with your mother," he speculated.

"No, Mom went to the movies with Tom," said Ayla.

Sebastian was unhappy that he didn't know where Elena was. He said goodbye to them and walked out of the entertainment room. He searched several areas where he knew she hung out but had no luck. He went to the security office and asked the guard to show him all the cameras. After they looked at all the areas with cameras he wasn't any closer to finding her. He paced the office frustrated and angry. He knew she wouldn't leave without saying goodbye to her family, so that meant she was still here.

He sat back on the chair, then pointed to the camera going into the woods, "I want to see the video for this camera from earlier tonight," he ordered.

The guard promptly used the computer to upload the video for Sebastian who watched the screen intently, keeping a look out for anything unusual. He checked the time. It was about two hours before dawn and he'd been watching the video for more than two hours before he thought he saw something. "Rewind just about two minutes, then slow it down," he requested.

The guard did as he asked, which enabled them both to see the shape of a person running into the woods. Sebastian watched for another few seconds until he had the exact direction she had taken. He rushed out of the security office and ran out of the house. He ran at extreme speed into the woods in the direction Elena had taken.

Sebastian saw her lying down on the grass, her face hidden by one of her arms. He kneeled down in front of her. "Elena," he called softly. "Elena," he called again, this time gently touching her arm.

Elena moved her arm from her face, opened her eyes and looked at him. She batted her eyelids twice, and when she focused her eyes and recognized him, she sat up right away. He could see the pain in her eyes when she realized who it was. "Sebastian, I'm sorry. I lost track of the time," she said shaking grass from her blouse.

"Elena, are you okay?" he asked reaching for her.

Elena pulled away from him and stood up as she brushed the grass from her pants. "I'm fine. I just needed some fresh air," she said moving away farther.

"We should get back. It's almost dawn," he said.

"Yes," she said starting to walk.

Sebastian caught up to her and walked by her side saying nothing. They walked in silence the whole way and reached the garden in no time. Elena took the path that would bring them to the kitchen.

Sebastian opened the door for her, and she walked through the kitchen and out the hall toward to the back stairs. She stopped and faced him, "I'm fine. I know my way to the room. Thanks for coming to get me," she said in an even tone.

Sebastian hesitated to let her go but stepped back and let her pass. Elena moved quickly up the stairs. He watched her go, shoved a hand through his hair then slammed it on the wall. All he wanted was to follow her, fold her in his arms and make love to her.

Iskra and Ayla were watching TV in the entertainment room when James came in and said, "Sebastian is back. He looks angry." "That means Elena's back too," said Ayla. Iskra and Ayla quickly stood up and left the room. Elena heard a soft knock on the door. She got up from the bed and opened the door. "Mom, Ayla," she said with a warm smile as she let them in.

They followed her to the sitting area. Elena sat down on one of the chairs while the other two sat together on the sofa. "Are you okay, honey?" asked her mother.

"I'm fine, Mom," she said. "I'm sorry."

"For what?" asked Ayla.

"You two will be fine here. Sebastian will protect you. He's a great king. You're happy here, right Mom?" she asked. Ayla could tell that she was trying hard not to cry.

"Yes," her mother assured her.

"Good" Elena said, "I'm tired. We'll talk soon, okay?" she said standing up.

"Sure, honey," said her mother, standing up too and giving her a soft kiss on the cheek.

"You know I love you," whispered Ayla in her ear as she hugged her.

"Me too," said Elena. She walked them to the door and let them out. Ayla and Iskra looked at each other with deep concern.

Sebastian was on his third shot, but nothing could take away the anguish he was feeling. He swallowed the shot then slammed the glass on the bar. He looked to the far side of the room where he saw Iskra and Ayla walking over to James and Matt. As he watched them talking, Ayla jumped in Matt's arms and began to cry. He didn't like what he saw and rushed over to where they were.

Sebastian approached them, "What's wrong?" he asked her.

"She's leaving us," said Iskra in a sad voice.

"She told you that?"

"No, but it was the way she talked. She assured us that you would take care of us, then she said she would talk to us soon. Mom's right, she's leaving," said Ayla with tears in her eyes.

"No she isn't," Sebastian said turning around and rushing out of the room.

Elena shut the water off, but she couldn't stop the tears from coming. She slid her body down the wall and sat down holding her knees tightly to her body. She hid her face on her knees and kept crying. Her sobs were loud now; she shook all over.

Sebastian opened the door and walked into his room. He didn't see her but noticed that the bathroom door was open. He walked into the bathroom and saw her sitting in the stall crying with her head down. His heart broke as he listened to her sobs.

Sebastian walked over to the stall, "Elena, babe," he said reaching for her.

"No, don't," she said pushing his hands away.

"Elena," he said wrapping an arm under her legs and back and pulling her up. Elena fought him but he just held her body closer to his chest. She stopped struggling. He sat on the edge of the bed with her on his lap. "Sebastian, let me go," she said with sadness in her voice.

He pulled strands of wet hair from her face. "Elena, what's wrong?" he asked.

She hid her face on his chest and started to cry again. "I saw you going into Klara's room," she said sharply, "I can't do this. I can't watch you mate with Klara. I don't want to be your mistress. I want more."

"Elena, I'm sorry. I didn't mean to hurt you." Sebastian could feel that she was cold so he pulled the blanket off the bed and wrapped it around her shoulders. He put his hand under her chin, pulled it up and forced her to look at him. Tears still streamed down her face. "Elena, you've been frustrating me to no end, but now I know I should have told you."

"Told me what?" she asked.

"That I have no intention of mating Klara. Julian is mating her instead." Elena looked at him with a puzzled expression.

"From the moment I saw you, I knew you were the only one for me."

"So why were you in Klara's room?"

"Klara was helping me."

"With what?"

"I asked her to order a dress for you."

Elena straightened on his lap, "A dress?"

"Yes, a mating ceremony dress. Elena, I want to mate with you."

His statement shocked Elena. Her heart beat faster and her body began to shake. "Why?" she asked in a whisper.

He looked into her eyes and could see hope there. He stroked her lower lips with his thumb and brushed the back of his hand on her cheek. "Because I love you," he declared.

"Sebastian, please don't tease me. I'm no one," she said.

"You're someone to me. You brought happiness and love to my life," he said giving her a soft kiss on the lips.

"Me too, I didn't want to love you because I was so sure I wasn't going to survive the assignment. I was so scared."

"Say it again," he said smiling at her.

"I love you," she said smiling back at him.

Sebastian hugged her tighter to his body then lowered his head and captured her lips. Elena wrapped her arms around his neck and opened for him. He thrust his tongue into her mouth. They launched into an exciting duel exploring every corner of each other's mouths. He stopped the kiss and settled her back on the bed. He stood up and quickly took off his clothes.

Elena scooted over and made room for him as she gave him a big smile. He climbed into the bed and slid under the blanket with her. He covered her body with his as she wrapped her arms around his neck and pulled him down for a kiss. That kiss was the beginning of the most amazing hours of lovemaking.

They lay back on the bed, breathing hard and tangled in each other's arms. She snuggled against him and rested her head on his chest. Sebastian watched her for several minutes as her breathing slowed down. When he knew she was asleep, he closed his eyes too.

Chapter Eighteen

Elena woke up but didn't open her eyes. Her body had an exquisite buzz all over. Their lovemaking hours before was amazing; her body felt satisfied and her heart was happy. After a few seconds, she realized that Sebastian wasn't with her in bed. She opened her eyes, looked around the room and listened for sounds in the bathroom. She threw the blanket off and slid out of bed. As she was walking into the bathroom, she saw a piece of paper on the nightstand.

She picked it and read it out loud, "Duty calls. Guests arriving. I have to greet them. Sorry. Love you." Short and to the point, she thought.

She put the paper back on the nightstand and went in the bathroom for a quick shower. Within ten minutes she was back in the room getting dressed. She chose a simple casual dress and comfortable but elegant shoes. She pulled her hair into a bun and applied a bit of makeup.

She picked up her phone to check for messages and phone calls from the office. She responded to one from her direct manager, then shut it off. She checked herself in the full-size mirror on the wall; happy with the results, she walked out of the room. Just as she was starting to walk down the stairs, her mother and sister approached her. She gave them a big smile.

"Mom," she said hugging her and giving her a kiss on the cheek. She moved to her sister and did the same.

"Is everything okay?" asked her sister as she let her go.

"Yes."

They both smiled back at her and together all three of them walked down the stairs. As they came down, she could hear several groups of people chatting and laughing in the living room, plus a few small groups in the foyer. She didn't feel comfortable socializing with anyone. The entire time she had spent in the mansion she never got close to anyone except Julian and Klara.

She decided that it was best if she stayed out of the way. She walked into the living room with them but then smiled to her mom and sister and made her excuses. From the corner of her eye she saw Sebastian and Julian talking to a group of men. She walked opposite to the group and made her way towards the terrace doors.

Sebastian was talking to Klara's father and three of the pack leaders. "Excuse me," he said to the group as he walked towards her.

Elena kept her head straight. She was so focused on getting out that she didn't sense him coming. As she lifted her hand to grab the doorknob, she saw him standing beside her. "Hi," he said with a big smile on his face.

"Hi," she said back.

"Come. I want you to meet some friends."

"Sure."

He took her hand in his and walked back to the group with her by his side. Elena knew she was attracting looks from people and it made her a bit nervous. He let go of her hand and wrapped his arm around her waist, pulling her closer to him. "Hi, everyone. This is my fiancée Elena. Elena these are pack leaders, Jeff, Steve, Mike and Klara's father, Bob," he said introducing her to them.

"Hi," she said as she shook everyone's hand.

"So you're the lady who captured the king's heart," one of the leaders observed.

"Yes," she said shyly.

Sebastian held her close as he resumed his conversation with the leaders. Elena stood next to him just listening. A few minutes later, Klara approached the group.

"Gentlemen, Elena, father," she said smiling, "I'm going to steal Elena for a bit," she said taking Elena's elbow.

"I asked Klara to help you with your things for the ceremony tomorrow," Sebastian said looking at her then letting her go.

"Sure," she said as she walked away from him.

Her mother and sister joined them as they walked into the foyer. "Where are we going?" she asked.

"To my room," answered Klara.

All four walked up the stairs and down the hall to Klara's room. Klara opened the door and let them in. Immediately Elena saw the two ceremony dresses inside the closet. She hesitated for a moment then walked to the closet. Hanging there was the same dress that Klara had asked her to try on the last time they went to the dress shop for Klara's final fitting. Klara insisted that she to try on several dress, and the dress in the closet was the one Elena had fallen in love with.

"Sebastian asked me to get you everything you needed. Here," she said handing her a large box. Elena held onto the box looking at everyone.

"Open it," said her mother.

"C'mon, open it," her sister urged.

Elena placed the box on the bed, pulled the top off and flipped the tissue paper out of the way. She stared at everything in the box.

"Sweetie, let's see it."

Slowly she pulled everything out. She set out on the bed a very pretty silky white bra and thong. Then she pulled a soft, white pink garter. Then she opened a shoebox to find the heels she had also tried on that day. She pulled out a small box and opened it. "It's so beautiful," she said looking at the sapphire necklace and earring set.

"That belonged to Sebastian's mother," Klara said.

The last thing in the box was the veil. As she pulled it out, she recognized it as her mother's from the pictures of her parents' ceremony.

"Mom, it's beautiful. Thank you," she said giving her a hug.

Elena looked at them and a tear rolled down her cheek.

"Honey, are you okay?"

"Yes, it's a happy tear."

They stayed for a while in the room talking about the ceremony. Elena knew everything about the ceremony process having been a planner for many years. They sat down chatting and laughing until they heard a knock at the door. Klara stood up and opened the door.

"Sebastian, Julian," she said letting them in.

Sebastian connected with Elena's eyes and quickly walked over to her. He took her hand and pulled her into his arms.

"Thank you," she said. "Everything is beautiful."

"You're welcome," he said beaming at her.

"We're just letting you know that the group insisted on taking us out for some drinks," Julian said, wrapping an arm around Klara's waist.

"Okay," she said.

"Great, we can make this a ladies' night," said Ayla.

"Definitely," said Klara.

"We better go. They're waiting for us. I'll see you later," Sebastian said, giving Elena a quick kiss on the lips.

Julian gave a soft kiss to Klara too and together the brothers walked out of the room. The ladies went back to chatting as they put everything back in the box. Elena picked up the box while Ayla took the dress from the closet. They walked out of Klara's room and down the hall into Elena's room. After putting everything in the closet, Elena and the other three walked down to the entertainment room. All four got a mixed drink and walked down the hall to the back of the mansion and out to the garden. Elena picked out benches where they all sat down and talked while they sipped their drinks.

The night was perfect. It was the end of the summer and it was cooler at night. They sat talking until all of them finished their drinks. "Time for another drink," said Ayla as she stood up from the bench.

"Yes," agreed Iskra.

They walked back to the mansion and went back to the entertainment room where they all got a second drink.

Elena saw that the pool table wasn't being used, "Let's play a game," she suggested.

"Yes," said Klara.

"Okay," said her mother and sister together.

They moved to the pool table and ended up playing three games. After the third, they all decided to call it a night. They said good night and walked up to their rooms. Elena decided to go to her room instead of Sebastian's. She took her clothes off and put on a spaghetti-strap camisole and men's boxers. She shut off the light and climbed in bed.

Elena closed her eyes. Recent events seemed completely unreal to her. She came to Louisiana to plan the king's ceremony and get her family away from Arnav and to safety. She never dreamed she would fall in love with the king and she definitely didn't imagine she would be getting mated to him. Happy tears dropped down her cheek as she smiled to herself. She got comfortable and tried to sleep.

Elena woke up slowly. She could sense someone moving around in her room. She readied herself for the assault she knew would be coming. She waited until she knew from which direction he would attack, and then she spun away from the charge and quickly positioned herself on top of the bed facing her attacker with dagger in hand. She didn't give him enough time to react, but launched herself at him. They fought for several minutes with Elena on the offensive the entire time. The other vampire barely escaped her slashes, but she had managed to slow him down with a few small cuts.

"Who are you?" she asked.

"The King killed my brother. He was only following orders from Arnav. Now I will kill you." She jumped at him again, this time leaving him with a large slash in his chest.

The vampire backed away from her and touched his chest, feeling the blood pouring from the wound. He looked around for a way to get out. The only opening was the balcony door, which was opened slightly. He rolled over the bed, ran out to the balcony and jumped to the ground.

Elena ran after him, jumping behind him and keeping on his heels. He ran through the garden and into the woods. She picked up speed, keeping him in sight. He was losing speed because he was dripping blood; Elena was catching up to him.

Sebastian was glad to be back at the mansion. He said goodnight to everyone and rushed up to his room. As soon as he entered the room he knew she wasn't there. He closed the door and walked to Elena's room. When he walked in he could immediately see that there had been a struggle in the room.

Sebastian found blood on the sheets and screamed for Julian. Julian rushed into Elena's room and, like his brother, he instantly could see that there had been a struggle.

"Fuck," he yelled.

"What happened here?" asked one of the leaders who was standing behind Julian.

"There is blood on the bed. Can you smell which way they went?" asked Sebastian.

Julian moved swiftly to the bed, "This is not her blood," he observed.

"I know. Which way?" Sebastian demanded.

"Out the balcony," said Julian.

"Put the house on alert. I want every vampire accounted for," he ordered Bob.

"Yes, my king."

Sebastian turned around and immediately he and Julian jumped to the ground and Julian started to track the blood smell. Sebastian ran behind his little brother. They only had to run for a few miles before they saw her fighting the vampire.

In the woods, Elena sprang onto the vampire's back and together they rolled on the ground. He flipped her off of him; she rolled and stood back up quickly to resume her fighting position. He was breathing hard, holding his side. They circled each other.

"Elena," screamed Sebastian.

She didn't react to his scream, but the other vampire did. She kept her eyes on the other vampire who was now visibly nervous.

"He's mine," she said firmly.

Sebastian moved towards her, but Julian grabbed his arm and stopped him. "Don't, let her finish it," he said.

Elena moved slowly, shifting her weight to her back foot. Suddenly, she leapt into the air and landed behind the vampire, quickly pulling his head back to expose his neck, she swiftly slashed his head off. She moved away and let the body and head drop to the ground where they instantly turned to ashes.

Sebastian rushed to her and wrapped her in his arms. He pulled her tight against his body. He let her go for a moment, pulled his shirt off and helped her put it on. "Let's get out of here," he said starting to walk away.

Julian walked beside them, "Who was that?" he asked.

"He said his brother was one of Arnav's man. He wanted revenge for his death," she said calmly.

"Are you okay? He didn't hurt you?" asked Sebastian.

"I'm fine," she said.

They walked silently back to the house. As she entered the living room, Iskra and Ayla together with James and Matt rushed to her.

"Go to your family, I have matters to attend to," Sebastian said, giving her a quick kiss on the lips.

"Don't leave her alone," he ordered firmly to all four.

They all nodded to him. Elena went with her mother to a large sofa where she sat down between her mother and sister.

"Are you okay, honey?' asked Iskra.

"I'm fine, Mom," she answered.

Elena watched as Sebastian, Julian and the other leaders walked out of the room. She looked around to see several guards positioned around the room. She stayed quiet for a few seconds then started to tell them what had happened.

Sebastian walked up the stairs to a large conference room where he sat down and waited for the rest of the group to sit down. He was furious that another assassination had been attempted. And this time the target was his fiancé—that just wasn't acceptable.

"How did this happen—again—in my own house?" he yelled furiously, slamming his hand on the table.

"My lord, Pete has been with us for more than a year. There was no indication that he knew the two vampires from Europe," said Tom.

"Did we do a background check on him?" he asked Tom.

"Yes, he came to us with excellent references."

"Fine. I want an extensive investigation on everyone in the house," he ordered.

"Yes, sire."

"Julian, I want extra security, plus bring a team in for the ceremony. I won't allow any more attempts on our lives," he ordered.

After discussing the matter with the leaders for several minutes, they all agreed on the next steps to take and quickly finished the meeting.

Dawn was approaching so it was time for them to go to sleep. Everyone left the conference room and found their way to their rooms.

Sebastian and Julian walked back downstairs. Julian went to his office to attend to the last-minutes changes in security.

Sebastian walked into the living room where Elena was still with her family. "Ready to get some rest? We have a ceremony tomorrow."

"Yes," Elena replied.

Sebastian offered her a hand, she took it and he pulled her up from the sofa. "Goodnight," he said to everyone and walked away with her.

In a matter of minutes they were in his room with her in his arms as he devoured her lips with his. Elena opened her mouth for him and he thrust his tongue in. He continued to kiss her, savoring her mouth.

"I was so scared," he said breathlessly. "I thought I was going to lose you."

"Never. You're stuck with me," she said laughing.

"I love you," he said.

"I love you too," she replied.

"It's been a rough night, plus we're going to be busy tomorrow night," he said lifting her in his arms.

"I need a quick shower," she said smiling at him.

"Fine, let's shower together," he said walking towards the bathroom.

He put her down. Elena took a step back and removed her clothes while Sebastian did the same. She moved to the stall and started the water. Sebastian moved behind her and walked into the stall. He grabbed the washcloth, poured gel on it and started to wash her. Elena leaned into his touch. He finished washing her body, then moved on to her hair. He rinsed her quickly then washed and rinsed himself.

He shut off the water and walked out of the stall, pulling her along with him. They both dried off quickly, then he lifted her in his arms. He walked back to the room and settled her on his bed then put on some underwear.

Sebastian covered her with the sheet then climbed into bed next to her. She cuddled next to him, putting her head on his chest and quickly closed her eyes. He held her tight, not relaxing until he could hear her breathing slow down. As soon as he knew she was asleep, he relaxed and closed his eyes too.

CHAPTER NINETEEN

SEBASTIAN AND ELENA WERE startled awake by the banging on the door. He moved quickly out of bed and pulled the door open, ready to yell at whomever the hell was making so much racket. When he looked he could see three smiling women by his door.

"Klara, what the hell do you think you're doing?" he asked, standing at his door with only his briefs on.

"It's ceremony night, remember? We need to get ready," she said in a perky voice holding a dress and box.

Next to her was Iskra and Ayla already dressed. Ayla also held a dress and box. They all stood there, smiling at him.

"Fine, give me a minute," he said trying to close the door but with no luck as Klara stood in the doorway not moving.

He moved from the door, grabbed his pants from the floor and put them on. He could see that Elena was trying very hard not to laugh.

"Your things are in Julian's room," said Klara already inside the room.

He walked over to Elena who was still lying in bed, gave her a quick kiss on the lips and left the room. Iskra and Ayla had been waiting patiently outside, but as soon as he passed them they rushed into the room.

Walking down the hall he could hear them laughing. He got to his brother's room and walked in. He could hear Julian in the bathroom. He opened the balcony and walked out.

He could see from there the intense activity down in the garden. The chairs and platform for the mating ceremony were already set up and illuminated with festive lights. On the other side of the garden he saw the big tent for the reception celebration also sparkling with light. The gardens were all lit up and decorated beautifully. Elena had done a fantastic job with the ceremony planning.

"Hey big brother," said Julian walking out of the bathroom with a towel wrapped around his waist.

"Hi," Sebastian said walking back in the room.

"Everything looks beautiful. Elena did a great job."

"Yes, she did."

"Your turn," he said pointing to the bathroom.

Sebastian walked past him into the bathroom. Sebastian came out of the bathroom as Julian was putting on his tuxedo "Your things are on the sofa," Julian said.

"Thanks," Sebastian said, walking over to the sofa.

Within a half an hour both men were completely dressed. They worked on their hair, both having tresses a bit past their shoulders. Sebastian pulled his hair back and wrapped it in a leather thong, while Julian left his loose. They checked each other out to make sure they didn't miss anything and both walked out of the room. They went downstairs to the living room, where some of the leaders were already gathered. They all shook hands and stood around talking.

They went down to the living room, watching as the guests started to arrive and were escorted to the ceremony area. Sebastian paced the room anxiously; he never felt so nervous in his life. Having Elena in his life was the greatest thing that had ever happened to him.

He checked his watch; it was only a few minutes until the ceremony. He went and stood next to Julian. After several minutes, an elder vampire who was performing the ceremony approached them. "Ready sire, Julian?" he asked.

"Yes," they both said.

"Then let's get you two mated," he said walking out onto the terrace with Sebastian and Julian behind him.

The rest of the leaders and pack members came out. The elder told them where to stand then positioned himself in front of them to wait for the ladies.

Back in Sebastian's room, Elena and Klara had just finished doing their hair and now were applying their makeup with the help of Iskra and Ayla. After they were done with their makeup, Iskra helped Klara with her dress while Ayla help Elena with hers.

Elena was all nerves. She paced the floor, not daring to leave the room. The rest of the women had been trying to soothe her and coax her out of the room for several minutes, but they were having no luck.

I love him too much—that's the problem, she thought to herself staring at the ladies in a panic.

She moved to the balcony and looked down at the big crowd in the garden. Her palms began to sweat as she walked back into the room still looking outside at the night.

"Elena, sweetie, what's wrong?" asked Iskra.

Down in the garden, Sebastian and Julian looked at each other. They had been waiting for more than thirty minutes. "What do you think is wrong?" asked Julian moving next to his brother.

Sebastian didn't answer right away then he said, "Elena."

"Go to her," he said.

Sebastian walked swiftly past the crowd waiting in their seats, into the house and up to his room.

Upstairs, Elena heard Iskra's question but didn't know how to answer. She was silent for a few seconds before she said with a shaky voice, "I'm scared. What if I'm not the right woman for him?"

"Elena," Sebastian said appearing suddenly behind the ladies. He walked by them and up to her, taking both her hands in his, "You're the only one for me, babe. I love you," he said smiling at her.

"I love you too," she said back to him.

"Then, let's get mated, okay?" he said as he took her hands to his lips and pressed a soft kiss on each palm.

"Okay," she said smiling back.

"I'll wait for you outside," he said giving her a quick kiss on the lips then rushing out of the room.

Elena looked at the ladies and smiled at them.

"Can we go now?" asked Klara.

"Yes," Elena replied.

All four of them walked out of the room, downstairs and out to the garden. Iskra and Ayla left them and found their seats next to Matt. They sat down and waited for the ceremony to begin.

Klara was joined by her father, while Elena was joined by James. Elena insisted that Klara go first. Slowly, Klara walked down the aisle with her father and a few feet behind them, Elena followed with James. Elena kept her eyes on Sebastian the whole time.

As they approached the platform, Bob took Klara's hand and offered it to Julian, then James gave Elena's hand to Sebastian. They settled into their positions and the elder started the ceremony.

Elena barely remembered the ceremony, but she did remember saying I do. She smiled at Sebastian as they walked down the path to the gardens where she knew the photographer was set up to take some photos of the couple and family. She held his hand tight, still nervous about all this attention. She couldn't believe she was mated to him. They arrived at a pretty garden full of flowers all lit up where the photographer put them in position and started to take the photos.

While they were getting their photos taken, the guests were escorted through the gardens to the large tent for the reception. Everyone was smiling and chatting away. Some gathered to chat with their friends while others found their seats and sat down.

After the photo session, the group walked together to the tent. As they got ready to enter, Sebastian bent down and gave her a quick kiss on the lips.

After the family members walked into the tent, the band played the ceremonial music and Julian and Klara walked in first followed by Sebastian and Elena. Everyone in the tent stood up and applauded the couples. They walked all the way to the main table where their family members were standing, waiting for them. They all sat down and the reception started.

Elena smiled to everyone; she was in a daze for most of the reception. She was so happy to be with Sebastian. She remembered doing all the things that were required of her for the ceremony, and now she found herself walking away from the reception area to the front of the house where there was a car waiting for them. "Where are we going?" Elena asked Sebastian.

"On our honeymoon," he answered.

"Honeymoon, really?" she said in a surprised voice.

"Yes, really," he said smiling to her and opening the car door.

Elena climbed into the car and scooted over to let Sebastian slide in beside her.

"Where are we going?" asked Elena.

"It's a surprise, babe," he answered.

He pulled her onto his lap and brought his lips to hers for a kiss. Elena wrapped her arms around his neck. He nipped and pulled on her lower lip. She opened for him and he launched his tongue into her mouth. They kissed for a long while, savoring each other. She laid her head on his shoulder and looked into his eyes. "Thank you," she said.

"For what?" he asked.

"For a wonderful night. I love you."

"I love you, babe."

He kept her on his lap for the rest of the drive. She held tight to his arms. She couldn't stop smiling and thinking about what a surreal night this was for her.

After another ten minutes, they arrived at the small airport. The guard opened the door for them. Sebastian climbed out before her, holding her hand and helping her out. With a guard on each side, they walked to the private plane and climbed the steps. Sebastian escorted her to the front of the plane and they settled into two very comfortable seats.

"Wow, this is beautiful," she said.

He grabbed her hand and brought it to his lips. A few minutes later, the pilot put the seatbelt sign on. They clicked their seatbelts and sat back as he took her hand in his. Soon the plane took off.

"I'm sorry," Elena said looking at him. "I should have told you about Arnav's plan. I was so scared for Mom and Ayla."

"Yes, you should have, but I understand why you didn't. We're together now—that's the important thing," he said caressing her face.

She leaned into his caress and closed her eyes. They sat quietly for a bit just holding hands. After the plane was in the air for some time, the seatbelt sign went off. Sebastian unclicked his seatbelt and helped her with hers. Then he pulled her up and sat her on his lap. "Maybe we shouldn't do this," she said looking around the plane.

"Don't worry, no one will bother us until I say so," he said.

She smiled and snuggled against his chest. He wrapped his arms around her waist and pulled her closer. They stayed together for a few minutes until he decided to request refreshments. He picked up the service phone and called for drinks and appetizers. After a few minutes, the attendant came out with what he requested and set up everything on the table in front of them. They ate some of the food and finished their drinks. Elena settled her head on his chest and closed her eyes. Minutes later, she was fast asleep.

She woke to Sebastian calling her name softly, "Elena."

She opened her eyes, "Are we there?"

"Not yet, but the plane has to land to refuel. You need to get back in your seat," he said.

"Oh, okay."

Elena moved to her seat and buckled her seatbelt. As soon as the plane landed they both stood up to stretch their legs.

"I need to use the bathroom," she said.

He walked her to the bathroom and waited for her. Then he went in. Elena stood by waiting for him. Before going back to their seats Sebastian asked the attendant for drinks. The seatbelt sign came on, they buckled up and a few minutes later the plane took off again to their final destination. They passed the remainder of the flight chatting and laughing. Finally the pilot announced their arrival and the plane started to descend.

They got off the plane and climbed into a car that was waiting for them. They waited a few minutes until their luggage was put in the car.

"Where are we?" she asked.

"We're in Paris," he answered.

"Paris, really?" she said smiling.

"Really."

"Thank you," she said throwing her arms around his neck and capturing his lips for a kiss.

He let her take the lead on this kiss, opening his lips for her. She launched her tongue into his mouth. He tucked his arm under her butt and lifted her onto his lap. They were still kissing as the car drove off. Elena settled back on his lap and enjoyed the drive.

A half hour later, they arrived at the hotel. The guard opened the door for them and they went to the front desk. They registered and got on the elevator. The attendant opened the suite for them, brought the luggage in and left the room. The guards checked the room then left them alone.

Sebastian scooped her in his arms and walked straight to the bedroom. He stood her up in front of him as Elena kicked her shoes off. He turned her to face the bed and slowly pulled her dress zipper down, while softly kissing her back. He finished with the zipper then went back up pushing her dress from her shoulders and making a trail of kisses from one shoulder to the other, stopping for a little nibble at her neck.

Elena moaned her approval. She wriggled her butt close to his crotch feeling his erection. He pushed her dress down to her waist and Elena pulled her arms out and let her dress drop to the floor. She kicked the dress to the side as he continued kissing her neck and shoulders.

Sebastian stepped back from her and slowly took his clothes off. Elena sat on the edge of the bed and pulled her thong off as she watched him with hungry eyes.

He grabbed her by her butt and lifted her up. She wrapped her legs around his waist as he devoured her lips and they gave each other hard thrusts of their tongues. They kissed for some time, then he crawled into the bed, keeping a hold of her with one arm and continuing to kiss her. Slowly he lowered them both onto the bed. He kept part of his weight off her by propping himself up with an elbow.

He stopped kissing her, lowered his head to her collarbone and started a trail of kisses down to her breasts. Elena slowly caressed his arms and shoulders while he tasted her nipples.

He continued teasing and nibbling for a while, then slid a hand down to her mound, slowly opening her pussy lips and sliding a finger between them. He took a nipple in his mouth and twirled his tongue around it, taking gentle nips.

Elena watched his every move, feeling all kinds of delicious sensations running through her body as he touched her. She pushed her hips up to feel his fingers, which were now inside her. He thrust in and out while alternating breasts. He kept up this delicious attack on her for several minutes, then he pulled his fingers out and stopped sucking her nipple. He rolled them over gently, putting her on top of him. "Take me inside you, babe," he murmured.

Elena pulled her hips up, moved her hand between them and took his shaft in her hand. She positioned it at her pussy entrance and slowly took him inside her. Sebastian held her hips with his hands. The deliberate way she was pushing down on him was pure torture, but he let her set the pace. Her body shook with the need of him; she took more of him, then moved faster and suddenly shoved down hard taking all of him inside her.

Elena gasped for air. The sensation of him stretching her completely was fantastic. She kept moving up and down as she swayed her hips back and forth. She was ready to come but wanted this to last longer.

With one hand, Sebastian pushed his hair off his neck and tilted his head to the side, offering his neck for her to take his blood. She eagerly lowered her head and as she rocked her hips forward and bit into his neck, drinking his blood.

"Yes, babe," he said in a husky voice.

Sebastian held her hips tight to his body and pumped hard and deep inside her. He kept the thrusts short and deep. Within seconds both burst into orgasm.

She stopped drinking his blood, licked the area and pulled herself up to feel all of him as their bodies continued to quiver.

She collapsed on top of his body. He wrapped his arms around her waist and held her tight against him. They stayed like this for some time. "That was amazing," she whispered in his ear.

"That's a good start, babe," he said flipping her over, still very hard inside her. He lowered his head and bit down on her neck and started drinking from her. "Sebastian," was all she could say as she exploded immediately in another orgasm.

After several hours of lovemaking, they settled in each other's arms, both completely satisfied and breathing very hard.

"I never thought I could be so happy," she said lifting her head from his chest.

"I love you," said Sebastian giving her a kiss on her forehead. With a big smile on his face he closed his eyes.

"I love you too," she said crossing an arm over his chest and laying her head on his chest.

She closed her eyes, also with a big smile on her face. She couldn't believe she was here in his arms as his mate. She remembered that when she came to Louisiana she was prepared to die, but her destiny changed when she crossed paths with him.

She thought to herself as she lay there, *Now I'm in the arms of my vampire, my king.*

THE END

TRUE DIRECTIONS
An affiliate of Tarcher Books

OUR MISSION

Tarcher's mission has always been to publish books
that contain great ideas. Why? Because:

GREAT LIVES BEGIN WITH GREAT IDEAS

At Tarcher, we recognize that many talented authors, speakers,
educators, and thought-leaders share this mission and deserve to be
published – many more than Tarcher can reasonably publish ourselves.
True Directions is ideal for authors and books that increase awareness,
raise consciousness, and inspire others to live their ideals and passions.

Like Tarcher, True Directions books are designed to do three things:
inspire, inform, and motivate.

Thus, True Directions is an ideal way for these important voices to
bring their messages of hope, healing, and help to the world.

Every book published by True Directions– whether it is non-fiction, memoir,
novel, poetry or children's book – continues Tarcher's mission to publish works
that bring positive change in the world. We invite you to join our mission.

For more information, see the True Directions website:
www.iUniverse.com/TrueDirections/SignUp

Be a part of Tarcher's community to bring positive change in this world!
See exclusive author videos, discover new and exciting books, learn about
upcoming events, connect with author blogs and websites, and more!
www.tarcherbooks.com

TRUE DIRECTIONS
AN AFFILIATE OF TARCHER BOOKS